This edition published 2020

This book is a work of fiction. All of the characters and character names are fictitious, and any resemblance to actual persons, living or dead, is purely coincidental.

Stories from The Garden

By

Andrew Millar

Index

<u>The Mystery Garden and the Magic Niger Seed</u>

Introduction

In the story in the following pages, the actions of the main character, Charlie, have a favourable influence on the events that unfold even although the situations he finds himself in are very difficult. I wrote the story from the perspective of a child as I believe a child displays a form of love that adults seem to lose as they mature, a love and tenderness that trusts in and cares for people even when they do not show the same in return. This is not to say we should be childlike but that we can learn from children through their sharing and interaction with us. Jesus said 'we must be childlike in our trust in God.'

The reason I wrote this story and the way it unfolds was to show that we must be good and positive role models in our lives, guiding, directing and teaching others how to live in love and to share and not to hate and be self-centred. I believe my faith in God helps me show this in my life and therefore my actions whether good or bad will reflect on this relationship I have with God and also people around me. We must always be careful that we don't give a bad or false impression of who we really are, as this will only create problems in the future.

We live and grow in family groups and share with other family groups as we are naturally dependent on one another to live our lives, whether we like it or not. Jesus taught us that we can never cure the whole world of wrong-doing but that we should do the best we can wherever we are.

Magic

'Charlie!!' a loud voice shouted from the far end of the garden shed. It was Charlie's father.

'What have I told you about moving and touching stuff in the shed?' Charlie's father continued sternly, not in anger, but more of frustration.

'Sorry, Dad,' Charlie responded sheepishly, but keen to show he wasn't misbehaving.

'I was only looking at this tub.' He held up a very large tub, trying to justify his actions – well, as Charlie was only 4 years old, the tub would have seemed large.

'What tub?' his father quickly answered, as he turned round to look in Charlie's direction.

'This one!' Charlie answered triumphantly, holding out the tub steadily towards his father.

His father had just finished cutting the grass and was in the middle of cleaning down his lawn mower in order to put it away.

'It says ni, nig, niger seed,' Charlie clarified.

His father turned round and looked towards Charlie.

'Guizotia abyssinica is its real name, but you can call it Niger seed,' his father explained.

'Be careful with it!' his father warned. 'That is the magic Niger seed.'

'Magic!!!' Charlie excitingly exclaimed with real triumph in his voice.

'Wow, real magic,' Charlie shouted.

'Yes,' confirmed the father. 'Magical indeed.' He smiled as he observed the excitement on Charlie's face. Charlie looked back at his father and grinned broadly, before asking, 'Magic – how?'

'Just be careful with it,' his father instructed as he tried to come up with some great story to keep his son interested. 'If you open it, the seed will disappear. Whoosh, gone!' His father laughed as a sudden worried look came across Charlie's face.

'You'd better put it back before you drop it,' he advised as he turned and moved the lawn mower towards the shed, having finished cleaning it down.

'Don't want us all to disappear, do you!' he asked, in a much firmer voice, trying to get Charlie to move out of the way so he could put the mower through the doorway.

Charlie looked at his father as he approached him, not really knowing what to believe. How could this tub be so dangerous, and in the shed? He turned thinking to himself, I'd better put it back, as I wouldn't want to disappear. Well, not before we have had tea anyway.

He put the Niger seed back onto the shelf. Imagine! Disappearing, never to be seen again, he thought.

After replacing the magic Niger seed on the shelf, he made his way into the garden. A quick check: everything all present and correct. All arms and legs, not to mention fingers are all still intact; phew. He was now safely back in the garden.

'Charlie.' A voice from the distance was calling him. It was Charlie's mother.

'Tea time,' she added. 'Time to come and get washed before tea,' she told him before disappearing back into the house.

Charlie duly ran towards the house, excited at the prospect of telling his mother what he had found; but also tea, food.

Charlie was Linda's and Richard's only child. As he was now 4 years old and a very inquisitive child, he was always asking all the usual questions, and making up stories with the things he had learned.

"Dad has magic ni-niger seed in the shed, mummy,' he exclaimed excitedly.

'Does he now!' she remarked with a smile on her face. 'Magic Niger seed indeed,' she commented, turning away so not to give the game away.

'Yes,' Charlie confirmed. 'Dad says we must keep it safe as it would be bad if we dropped it because we would disappear.' He put his hands up in a gesture to give the impression of a magic spell.

'Oh dear,' his mother responded. 'We can't have that now; can't have Charlie vanishing without a trace,' as she turned away trying not to laugh.

'Charlie never to be seen again; and before tea,' she remarked, speaking mysteriously and chasing after Charlie with her hands outstretched shaking her fingers up and down.

Charlie ran away screaming excitedly, trying to hide behind one of the dining table chairs.

'I hope you put it away safely,' she asked as he came towards her. She picked him up and gave him a hug and a kiss on his cheek.

'Yes, Mummy. I did,' Charlie answered returning the hug and feeling safe in his mother's arms.

'Ah good,' his mother replied. 'Now go and wash your hands and face before tea.' She said as she lowered Charlie to the floor.

'Okay, Mummy,' Charlie shouted as he ran off in the direction of the bathroom.

Linda moved toward the door and called: 'Richard, tea ready.'

'Coming,' a voice in the distance answered.

After tea the family went for a walk as usual down the little lane next to the house. On returning, Charlie's mother instructed him to change and get ready for a bath and then bed.

Charlie was a very obedient boy and duly ran off to his bedroom to change as his mother ran his bath.

Bedtime was always an occasion for stories. Sometimes his mother and sometimes his father would read him a story before he drifted off to sleep.

For the past few days it was his father who was reading him stories. He was reading a book which he had had and was read to him when he was a child.

After concluding the story, his father tucked Charlie in and gave him a little kiss on the cheek.

'Tomorrow night we will finish the last story in Granddad's story book,' his father explained.

'I like Granddad's stories,' Charlie responded enthusiastically.

'Yes, well,' continued his father. 'Not many people like these old stories anymore. They are all old news.' He sounded quite sad at the thought. 'They are good stories with real friends to me. But they are all gone! Nobody reads them anymore,' he added despondently as he rubbed his hands through Charlie's hair. 'Just as well we keep them alive by sharing them together,' he concluded 'Well, lad, time to sleep,' as he walked towards the door and switched off the light.

'Night, Charlie,' he said as he closed the door.

'Night, night,' Charlie responded.

Charlie lay there for a while thinking about the stories they had read over the last few days. What did his father mean by nobody reads them anymore? Where have they disappeared to? Maybe they had had the magic Niger seed and dropped it! His eyes started to get heavy trying to think it through, and before he knew it, he had dropped off to sleep.

Charlie Vanishes and Encounters a Rabbit

Just then he heard a scream.

'No Charlie! No.' it was his father's voice. They were back in the garden. He was holding the tub of magic Niger seed.

'Charlie, nooooo,' the voice faded away the moment Charlie dropped the tub to the ground and all the seed spilled out.

Charlie looked round to see his father, but it was no use - he was disappearing into a white mist, like a cloud vanishing with every second. There was nothing he could do. He was being whooshed away beyond his control.

'Daddy.' Charlie shouted, but it was no good. His father was nowhere to be seen. Charlie was alone, drifting away in some dark murky cloud. Where is this place? What am I to do, thought Charlie? His heart sank as he thought of his mother's words: "We can't have that now; can't have Charlie vanishing without a trace. Charlie never to be seen again; and before tea."

'Oh no!' Charlie heard himself shout.

Lots of questions rushed into his mind: Where is the garden, Dad and Mum? It's all gone. One moment it was there and now it's gone.... it's gone very dark, very heavy, all of a sudden alone! Where am I? This must be the magic Niger seed's magic!

‘Hey! Who are you? What are you doing here?’

Charlie, startled by the sudden shouting, turned round. Immediately, the darkness lifted, and there before him to his surprise was an old, large white rabbit towering over him.

‘What the . . .!’ The rabbit started to say in a very loud angry voice.

The rabbit stood over Charlie. He had an old broken pocket watch dangling from his jacket pocket. He was wearing what looked like the remains of an old pair of glasses as one had a cracked lens and the other lens was missing.

‘Come on, man. Explain yourself,’ the rabbit snapped.

Charlie noticed in the background an old rocking chair, still in motion. The rabbit must have been startled as he had clearly suddenly jumped up to confront Charlie.

Charlie stood up startled, not knowing how, where or what was happening; everything seemed to occur so quickly. . . and now to be challenged by a giant white rabbit.

‘Excuse me!!!’ the rabbit snarled. ‘Are you deaf, stupid or just down-right rude?’

Charlie tried to collect himself to take it all in. He gasped for sufficient breath to answer, but the rabbit once again raised his voice poking him now in the chest.

‘I was asking you a question,’ he shouted. ‘Come on man, answer!’

Charlie was startled by the rabbit's sudden abruptness. He stepped back and started to speak.

'I'm mm, Chr - arlie,' he stuttered.

'I'mmmmmmm Charrrrrliiiiieeee!!' The rabbit mimicked, making as much fun of him as he could.

'Charlie,' Charlie retorted.

'Well, why you couldn't have said that, rather than standing there with your big mouth open trying to catch flies,' the rabbit grumbled and sat back down in his rocking chair.

'You are one rude rabbit,' Charlie blurted out, feeling more at ease now that the rabbit had retreated to his chair.

'Me... Rude, me!!' The rabbit responded raising himself from his chair and leaning forward, gesturing and poking himself in the chest as he tried to defend himself from the sudden accusations. 'I was just sitting there minding my own business, rocking gently in my chair, enjoying a few moments of quietness, when you!' suddenly prodding Charlie in the chest.

'You, yes, you!' raising his voice as high as a rabbit can raise his voice. 'You just fell in right at my feet. No warning, no apologies, no thought of an old frail rabbit's health.' He paused for breath before continuing.

'Just downright rude, not to mention dangerous.' At this the rabbit seemed to stumble, whilst cheekily looking at Charlie to see if he showed any signs of guilt, remorse or concern.

'You never know the damage you could cause'.

The rabbit sat in his chair, at the same time holding his chest and wheezing, watching to see if Charlie would react to his play acting and be startled.

'After all,' he went on, 'an old hard-working rabbit like me can't take these sudden shocks by young rude whipper smackers like you!' He was beginning to get a little annoyed as Charlie seemed to be paying no attention to his, what he thought, was his Oscar-winning performance.

Charlie looked at him in bewilderment and tried to respond.

'I am very sooo...' he was cut off as he was trying to speak.

'And so you should be, you horrible little boy!' the rabbit snarled, by now irritated as Charlie appeared unfazed at his effort to elicit sympathy. However, he was delighted to think that he was winning the moral victory.

'Speak up, lad!' the rabbit snapped. 'You are a boy, aren't you? Have you lost your tongue......? boyyyy,' holding onto the 'y' a little longer than it was comfortable to hear. 'We don't get many visitors here, and then you, the village idiot boy, turns up! Ugh,' the rabbit squirmed. 'Well, not rude and horrible boy visitors like you, anyway,' ranted the rabbit, quite pleased with himself as Charlie remained quiet, overawed by all that was happening.

Charlie was at a loss for words. After all, how do you argue with a talking rabbit, especially one who will not let you get a word in?

'The last outside visitor we had here who looked like you was a lovely lass . . . mmm . . . her name was . . . ehhmm . . . Alice.' The rabbit was pleased with himself, having remembered the name.

'Yes, Alice was her name.' He looked intently at Charlie. 'Don't suppose you know her by any chance?' he questioned.

'No, no, no, of course not.' Charlie answered abruptly.

'No, she would never have anything to do with a rude little boy like you. Don't know what I was thinking!' He stopped and scratched his chin.

'You don't know her, do you?' he continued and then paused for a few seconds.

'No, of course not,' Charlie squirmed.

It was at that moment the penny dropped in Charlie's mind.

'Of course!' Charlie responded loudly.

'Alice in Wonderland!' he stated in triumph.

Now the rabbit was speechless, standing there and realising how the tables had turned. Charlie was now the one with the upper hand.

'Alice;' Charlie continued. 'I know Alice of course.' There was a slight pause and then he smiled at the questioning rabbit...

'Never met her though. But my Dad told me all about her and her visit here.'
The rabbit looked at Charlie with great excitement in a hurry to hear more. Charlie continued:

'My Dad did mention a rabbit that was always rushing about like a headless chicken.' Charlie laughed.
The rabbit fell silent and settled back into his chair.

'It couldn't be you as you seem to be a bit of a lazy rabbit rocking about on your chair.' Charlie was smirking as he realised the rabbit was now in shock at the turnaround in circumstances. However, within that few short moments the rabbit had managed to take a deep breath and regain his composure sufficiently to be able to respond.

'I haven't always been in this chair, you cheeky boy.' He gestured with distaste at the suggestion that he was the lazy one. Charlie on the other hand was delighted to have got his own back. It had been so easy to put the rabbit in his place. Trading insults seemed the only thing this rude rabbit understood.

'No, no, could never have been the same Alice!' the rabbit countered. 'She would not have kept company with the likes of you!'

The rabbit was now struggling to gain composure. On the one hand he wanted to trade insults with this intruder, and on the other hand he wanted to find out about Alice, wonderful kind-hearted Alice. Without thinking, the rabbit spoke in a calmer and much more collected tone. 'No, the place has never been the same since Alice left...'

There was a slight pause. 'Wonderland was a much happier place then. A truly wonderful place, brightened up with a lovely girl like Alice.'

The rabbit realised he had let down his guard. He cleared his throat and leaned towards Charlie. 'No, not like someone as rude and horrible as you are.'

Again the rabbit grasped his chest and sat back in his chair waiting to see if Charlie would respond sympathetically. Nothing happened. Charlie just stood there, feigning no interest.

'Wonderland was made more wonderful with Alice here. The rabbit sighed. 'But since she left everyone.... Well...' the rabbit went silent, staring into space.

He gathered himself together and continued: 'Everything seemed to change not long after she left! It became more like blunderland as everyone blamed everyone else for Alice having to leave.'

The rabbit looked visibly upset. 'The place went down-hill fast. It all faded overnight. No more tea parties, no more important dates, just emptiness.'

The rabbit sat back in his chair with what looked like tears in his eyes. Charlie felt sorry for him. The rabbit then muttered in a low voice 'Those were the days.'

Just as Charlie was feeling sorry for the rabbit, he was suddenly startled as the rabbit stood up and began another vicious attack. ‘That was before you came along. Your cheek and rudeness caused all this unrest! You are disturbing our lives with your unwelcome attacks.’ The rabbit gave a little snigger, as he looked away from Charlie knowing that he had indeed taken back the initiative with his latest onslaught of insults.

‘What did you say your name was?’ The rabbit snapped back at him.

‘Charlie, Charlie,’ Charlie responded.

‘Charlie Charlie! What kind of name is that, Charlie Charlie?’ The rabbit smirked.

‘Well Charlie Charlie!’ He leaned forward just a few inches from Charlie, causing Charlie to move back with the aim of getting out of the way.

‘Close the door as you leave,’ the rabbit laughed mockingly as he knew Charlie had been shocked by his response and he wanted to make him feel as unwelcome as possible.

Charlie wanted to retaliate. He stepped to the side, away from the approaching rabbit, moving towards the doorway. The door opened as he reached it. The door seemed to open out into a walled garden area. The doorway seemed quite small. In fact, if he wanted to go through the door, he would need to crawl through on his hands and knees. He moved towards the door. Charlie turned and was just going to speak when the rabbit shouted.

‘Good riddance to you, Charlie Charlie,’ scorned the rabbit. ‘Don’t come back,’ he shouted.

Charlie reached the doorway. He went down on his hands and knees as there was no point in trying to speak to the rabbit now that he was so aggressive. Charlie was about to move through the doorway when a much gentler voice said: 'If you see Alice in your travels, tell her to come back. We all miss her,' commented the rabbit, suddenly seeming to mellow as he sat back again in his chair.

'I will, Mr Rabbit,' Charlie responded. 'I promise I will.' Charlie moved to go through the door, feeling quite sad. At first he thought he would stay, but then he realised that the rabbit could become more abusive and he wouldn't be able to leave. He moved towards the doorway.

'Good lad,' said the rabbit, as he continued to rock in his chair.

Charlie reaching the doorway, glanced back at the rabbit, smiled and said 'Bye.'

'Bye, Charlie Charlie,' the rabbit answered.

Charlie moved forward, passing underneath the doorway expecting to reach the walled garden. Instead he found himself falling down a chute as he headed into an abyss of thick blackness. He tumbled and spun and then, eventually, splash!

The Land of the Little

Charlie found himself lying face down in the water, having taken a mouthful of sea water. He lifted his head and spat out the water, leaving his mouth tasting rather foul and salty. The water was halfway up his side. He turned his head to see just where he was. After all, a few moments ago he was in Wonderland speaking to a rabbit, but now he was lying flat out in salt water. He looked to the left and saw only a vast sea wave before him. But when he turned his head to the right, he saw what he could describe only as utter turmoil.

Water was wooshing over the land like a minor tsunami. Several tiny boats the size of small matchboxes were bouncing up and down in the water. He heard horns and sirens blaring - seemingly to him to be in the distance. There appeared to be complete chaos, entirely in contrast to the view on his left

Within the few moments of getting his bearings, a small boat about the size of his right hand bumped into his face.

'What the... .' Charlie screamed with fright at being struck unaware. After all, it isn't every day that you end up in a far-off sea that is causing complete havoc all around.

'Get out of the way, you…' a slight pause. 'You thing, you.' The voice sounded far away, but it clearly came from the small boat that had just hit him.

Charlie was surprised to see the boat was actually a miniature wooden warship and seemed to have people aboard. The ship looked set to go to war or something. The voice seemed to be coming from within that area. Charlie scanned the ship one more time.

‘Get out of the way you, whatever you are,’ the small man on the front of the ship shouted. It was difficult to hear him as he appeared to be far away.

Charlie saw the small man shout directly at him. He seemed to be about an inch or so tall. He continued to scream at Charlie: ‘Get out of the way, you big lump!!’ he yelled at Charlie. It did seem quite strange to Charlie that the man was more interested in trying to move past him rather than in why this giant was in the sea, obstructing their passageway.

‘You are letting them get away, you fool.’ The man on the ship sighed with frustration. It was then Charlie noticed that the gentleman was wearing some kind of military uniform.

The man put his hands on his hips and turned to look at the men on his ship and then turned back to face Charlie once again.

‘Who are you and what do you think you are doing, dropping in from the sky in this way?’ There was a slight pause but before Charlie could respond the man started to chastise him again. ‘You are blocking our vital sea lanes, you idiot.’

He was waving his right hand and his first finger seemed to be pointed directly at Charlie. ‘You are in serious trouble whoever you are,’ he concluded.

It seemed strange to Charlie that here was a situation where tiny people on a small boat were screaming at him and accusing him of all things when he must be like a giant lying directly in front of them. It was laughable that they were upset at him rather than being terrified of what lay before them.

'Answer me you, big lump,' the man shouted at the top of his voice. By this time Charlie had repositioned himself so he could look straight at the man who was chastising him. He looked to be a plump little man, wearing what appeared to be an officer's uniform, similar to what we could have seen in old films of times gone by with yellow braided lapels and brass buttons. He had a small bushy beard and was wearing glasses, which looked far too small for his plump face as they seemed to dig into his temples. His cheeks were quite red, but that could be with all the shouting. The man raised his arm once again to point at Charlie, and Charlie noticed that the yellow braiding went round the cuffs on his sleeve.

'Can you not understand me, you big fat lump.' He seemed not only frustrated but also angry at the turn of events.

'Just what do you think you are doing blocking our sea lanes?' he enquired. 'You just lie there thinking you own the place.'

He looked rather frustrated as he shook his head and occasionally glanced at his fellow crew in wonder. 'Come on then answer me, or, mm, I will be forced to take some aa . . . 'He stopped abruptly as it seemed to Charlie that the immensity of the situation had just struck him. After all, if he was about to threaten him with violence, just what could he do with what he described as a big lump, which vastly outweighed him and his crew.

'I am Ch . . . Charlie,' Charlie answered.

'It speaks,' the man shouted.

'At last, it can communicate.' He smirked but at the same time he seemed to step back a little as if he was now unsure of what his next move should be.

'So you are Charlie,' he responded. 'A right Charlie if you ask me.' He looked at his men encouraging them to laugh at his pun.

'Yes, I am Charlie,' Charlie confirmed. 'I am sorry if I have upset you.' Charlie tried to be polite and diplomatic given that he was lying soaking wet in sea water.

'Sorry, you say,' the uniformed gentleman responded. 'So you should be, landing out of the sky here uninvited.' He was waving his hands in an attempt to emphasize his statement.

'We will say no more about it . . .' he continued. 'Be off with you!! Get out of our shipping lanes and let us get on with our lives, you fat lump.' The man was beginning to be somewhat rude. Charlie thought that maybe the man wanted to appear as being totally in charge when it was quite clear that this fat lump was more than a handful and a threat to them all.

The man started to walk away down into his boat shouting instructions to his crew.

'Wait, wait,' Charlie said in the friendliest tone he could muster.

However, the man continued to shout instructions to the rest of the men on the battleship.

‘Wait!!’ Charlie repeated. ‘I just want to talk with you, please,’ he pleaded. Charlie shifted from lying down in the water to sitting upright. The crew and the officer ignored Charlie’s pleas as they turned the ship around and headed off towards the coastline.

Charlie was quite annoyed at the turn of events. Little boys are not in the habit of being ignored so, in a good little boy fashion, as he would do in his bath at home, he reached over and picked up what he saw as a small boat. Charlie found it to be much heavier than he expected, but regardless of that he brought the boat up towards his face and looked directly at the crew who were screaming in somewhat of a panic.

The officer immediately ran up to the bow of the boat and shouted directly at Charlie.

‘What the heck do you think you are doing?’ shouting at the top of his voice.

Charlie was quite amused at what was taking place. The crew were running about on the ship. A couple had jumped overboard willing to take their chances in the open sea whilst the officer was screaming at him. Charlie could hardly contain his laughter.

‘I demand you put us down at once . . ’ the officer bellowed. ‘At once you hear!!!’

He stood with one hand pointing straight at Charlie with the other hand grasping onto the side of the boat so he could remain upright. The instruction given was very much the same as his father's would have been so Charlie realised then that the situation was serious indeed.

However, Charlie was still annoyed. 'Or what??' he giggled.

The officer was very red in the face and could not say anything for his anger and annoyance at the ordeal.

'Put us down at once,' he reiterated, as he screamed instructions to his men as well as starting to direct threats at Charlie.

Charlie was quite amused at his actions. He thought the officer now looked a lot like the cartoon character, Captain Pugwash, although he had a much redder face.

'This is no laughing matter,' the officer cried whilst throwing a small object at him. Charlie looked closely at the small object. It was a tiny sword, no bigger than a little tact nail from his father's nail box.

'I will put you back in the water if you don't calm down and answer my questions,' Charlie bargained.

'If you don't put me down, I will declare a council of war!' the officer snapped back in a very shaky voice as the situation was way beyond his control and he knew it.

'War!' declared Charlie as he lifted his left hand out of the water and flicked a couple of water droplets onto the boat. The crew and everyone on the boat were at once splashing about in the boat, crashing into anything and everything in their way. Charlie burst out laughing at the sight of the scramble. The officer regained his composure and moved forward to confront Charlie one more time although now he was dripping wet.

'That is not funny. You could have drowned us all,' he spluttered. It was clear he was now terrified and at this point Charlie sensed that something was not right here.

The officer responded: 'This is a serious matter, a very serious matter and you don't care!' He tried to reach the softer side of Charlie adopting a compassionate tone. He was now standing in front of Charlie holding up his hands in a gesture. 'Ok, we surrender!' he conceded. 'Is that what you want?' he asked Charlie, who could sense the urgency in his voice.

'I am Edward Marshall, the third King of Lilliput,' he explained.

Charlie was astonished. 'Lilliput!' he queried, immediately thinking of the story his father had read to him, written by a man called Swift! Which one was it, he asked himself? 'Gulliver's Travels,' he exclaimed quite loudly.

'Gulliver,' the King confirmed. 'Our history tells of a Gulliver giant,' he explained before adding: 'My great, great grandfather was friends with a giant called Gulliver. We always thought it was a myth,' he said. 'Do you now this Gulliver fellow?' asked the King. 'Oh, no, couldn't be anyone you would know. He wasn't disruptive and a trouble-maker like you,' as he waved his right hand firmly from side to side to illustrate his comment.

Charlie was still taken aback by this sudden change of fortunes. His mind was drifting a little when he noticed he was allowing the ship to tip over slightly as he relaxed his hand. He quickly caught it with his left hand and straightened it up again. Once again the crew and the King were sent scrambling for their lives trying to hold to anything that would save them from falling over.

'This is quite enough!' the King shouted.

'Either let us down or finish us off here and now, as this must end,' he demanded. He was about to issue the instruction to abandon ship when Charlie lowered the ship down a little, straightened it up just above the water level. Charlie was quite excited by the turn of events. Gulliver's Travels, he thought. He loved that story when his father had read it to him. There was such excitement in the voices his Dad used. He then looked at the ship and at the terrified crew.

'I will let you down, Your King-ness, if you promise to be nice and speak to me without being nasty or threatening.' He paused, waiting for the King to answer. He felt quite happy with himself and really wanted a chance to speak to the King about Gulliver.

The King was delighted with how the situation was developing and perceived an act of compassion by this intruding giant. But also he was eager to hear what this Gulliver fellow had to say. He might not be a myth after all. He looked at Charlie, put his hand to his chain and scratched his beard, trying to look as statesman-like as he could.

'Right,' he responded and moved towards Charlie.

'If you agree to end hostilities, we will consider establishing a treaty with you,' he said, trying to appear in charge to his fellow crew, after all that is what kings do.

'If you stop threatening me and my people, we will be happy to speak,' he concluded, holding out his hand as if he wanted to shake on the proposed deal.

Charlie looked at him warmly and reached out his pinkie finger of his right hand, trying to hold the ship steady as it was beginning to feel quite heavy.

'If I put you down in your harbour over there, can we talk?' Charlie questioned.

'Put us down here and we will sail in,' the King responded. 'It will give us a chance to see what damage we have sustained on our way back to port,' he explained. 'Once we are safely in the harbour we can talk.' The King tried to sound as if he was the one dictating the terms. He came across as quite confident, but it was clear to all, he was, like his men, terrified about the whole incident.

Charlie lowered the boat slowly into the water. He avoided making abrupt moves in order not to create waves and sink the ship now that he had come to an agreement with the King. Once Charlie had lowered the ship safely in the water, the King shouted instructions and the crew (the ones that remained) immediately took action.

'Safe journey,' Charlie called as he let the boat go.

The boat seemed to be okay. It did not appear to be letting in water. Slowly but surely the ship turned and headed back to the port, the King continuing to give orders at the top of his voice. Within a few moments the boat was steaming in the direction of the harbour.

After the boat was a safe distance away, Charlie slowly sat up. He stood up and moved very gently towards land, hoping to be able to speak to the King at last.

On reaching the harbour, Charlie settled down on the banking. He tried to dry himself off a little given how long he had been lying in the water. It was a lovely sunny afternoon, which he had not noticed until now because of all the commotion.

A few minutes after he sat down, a small delegation arrived just slightly off to the right of him, next to a group of houses, one of which seemed to be the local tavern and another a fishmonger.

'Now what do you think you are doing interfering in our lives like this,' challenged a voice from the crowd. Charlie looked down at the crowd and saw that King Edward Marshal III was standing amongst the group looking straight at him. Charlie lifted his hand from his clothes, which he had been trying to dry, and shook his head. At that a wash of water jetted from his hair and onto the approaching delegation.

'Sorry, sorry,' Charlie apologised. Some of the crowd were soaked but luckily none of the water landed on the King as it reached only the rear of the approaching group.

'Pull yourself together, man!' the King shouted.

'Can you not see what a danger you are to us?' he bellowed.

'I am sorry,' repeated Charlie. 'I didn't realise . . .' he tried to explain.

'No, you wouldn't,' the King interrupted. 'People like you just interfere in things which do not involve you, and then cause absolute chaos wherever you go.' The King seemed delighted at how things seemed to have turned in his favour.

'Well, I, I . . .' Charlie stuttered, trying to make his point, but the King again rudely interrupted him. He was feeling quite on top and wanted to keep the upper hand.

'You are no better than that last interfering giant we had here!' he complained. 'Coming here and causing chaos; I don't know what to think!' the King smirked as he continued: 'What was his name now?' He paused as he tried to convey the sense that the last giant to visit was not much of an event, hoping that it would put Charlie on the defensive. The crowd reacted nearly in unison as they chanted: 'Gulliver.'

‘That’s the fellow,’ said the King, rubbing his chin. He was glad that his plan seemed to be working as Charlie looked a little lost for words. He turned round slightly, away from the King in order to wipe some water off his face.

‘Don’t turn away when I am talking to you,’ admonished the King. ‘That is quite rude.’ The crowd murmured in agreement.

‘I was jus. . .s . . .s . .’ Charlie tried to say, but the King interrupted him as he wanted to retain the upper hand.

‘Now don’t interrupt,’ the King said forcefully. ‘Charlie, you are no better than that last giant intruder who visited here, thinking he owned the place.’ The King was delighted with himself even though he knew that according to legend Gulliver had been well remembered in history, and he was hoping that, by using this approach, he would keep this latest intruder at bay. He continued: ‘He came here interfering in our business and then disappeared leaving the people to fix the shambles he left.’ He paused. The days of being an amateur actor were coming into play as he knew when to pause to give the best effect.

‘Well I . . .’ Charlie tried to get the words out, but somehow his tongue seemed to be twisted. Taking a deep breath, he continued: ‘I am sorry for any trouble I have caused.’ The crowd growled as if to say ‘So you should be.’ Charlie went on, explaining: ‘I didn’t choose to come here. I just sort of dropped in.' He shrugged his shoulders as if this would amplify his statement.

'Just dropped in.' The King laughed mocking Charlie and looking to the crowd for approval. 'Just dropped in,' he continued, just as Charlie decided he was going to say his words now and not be bullied.

'Well I nothing,' Charlie stated in a loud voice. 'Who is being rude now, not letting me say anything to defend myself?' Charlie leaned forward in a slightly threatening manner to put the King and the crowd in a defensive mode.

They all stepped back a little, clearly terrified. Several of the crowd at the back ran off in the direction of the tavern, not wanting to be part of anything that might ensue.

'One minute I was in Wonderland and the next here!' Charlie said raising his hands in the air. 'I didn't choose to be here. It just happened.' He aimed to be as convincing as possible but at the same time trying to recall the stories his father had told him.

The King regained his composure. 'Wonderland indeed!' he said under his breath. 'Maybe you can just disappear and threaten their livelihood rather than make our lives miserable with your interference.' The King stood with his hands on his hips looking rather pleased with himself.

'I would if I could,' explained Charlie. 'But I have no idea how to!' It was quite clear Charlie at this point was a little upset as he thought of home and what, where and if he would ever get back there.

'Humm,' the King responded, trying to appear sympathetic but at the same time patronising. 'We would be obliged in the meantime if you would cause NO more trouble.'

'I have not come here to cause trouble,' Charlie answered apologetically. 'I just want to go home,' Charlie admitted, feeling rather sad for himself at this point.

The crowd by this time was starting to feel a little sorry for this mass intruder, much to the displeasure of the King, who showed this by turning round and giving the crowd a rather nasty look.

'Home! Where is that?' The King asked.

'A long, long way away, I think.' Charlie responded, looking rather upset with the circumstances.

'Come on, lad,' the King stated. 'Pull yourself together.' 'Don't start getting all soppy now! You've done your bit and we are ready to help and forgive you for your rude interruption,' said the King, playing to the crowd. The crowd eagerly murmured in agreement.

'Everything will work out, lad. You wait and see.' The King turned to the crowd for support for that last statement. This they did, by some saying yea while others nodded their heads. Some of the men who had run away at the last outburst, had returned to join in with the rest of the crowd, sensing that hostilities had somewhat turned to a peaceful discussion.

‘Tea!’ The King exclaimed in a high-pitched tone. ‘The last giant liked tea if I remember,’ added the King joyously.

‘Would you like some tea?’ the King asked Charlie. The King clasped his hands together, an indication that someone in the crowd should go off and make some tea. Charlie nodded his head in agreement.

Charlie spent the next few days in the presence of the King and the people of the village listening to and sharing old stories.

However, the feeling of sadness stayed with him. He felt homesick, lost and forgotten.

It became clear to Charlie that all had changed when Gulliver arrived. Things had been good, but after he left everything went back to the way it was. Whilst he had been here, people had high hopes for a better future. But after he left, everything returned to its old ways. The people blamed it all on Gulliver, saying he was the cause of all the problems.

On several occasions Charlie had tried to find out if it would be possible for him to return the same way as Gulliver, but the question was always ignored or shunned.

One day the bell was rung in the harbour. This was a warning sign for the entire village.

Everyone ran all the way down to the harbour to see what the reason was for the warning bell.

‘What’s going on?’ Charlie enquired.

‘A boat in trouble,’ the King explained.

Charlie stood up from his crouched position, his usual posture whilst with the villagers.

As he stood up, he could see in the distance a tiny boat listing in the water, clearly in danger. It looked as if it would overturn. Charlie took several large steps to move into the sea, which at the most would come up only to his knees.

A couple of small boats had started out from the harbour on their way to give assistance. But Charlie was well ahead of them, having got there in no time at all. He leaned down and saw the small fishing boat sinking into the water. He put his hand down below the small boat and scooped it out of the water. He then lifted the boat up in his hands and turned around and headed back towards the shore. Charlie lowered the boat onto the shore saving everyone on board, much to the delight of all the people on the shoreline.

Just then Charlie felt something stirring at his feet. Without warning the sand below his feet in the sea gave way and he plunged down below the water into what seemed to be a water slide.

It seemed to Charlie he tumbled and fell through what felt like a sinkhole, plunging through the sink down into water tubing. Eventually he saw light at the end of the tunnel.

It seemed so dark. He was spinning round and round. Maybe this is what it is like in a washing machine, he thought. There was a light still in the distance, then suddenly a bump.

He came to an abrupt stop. He landed on a hard surface. Everything around seemed overgrown; above the trees was a blue sky. But then darkness came over Charlie, as he dropped into a deep sleep.

The Yellow Brick Road

Eventually Charlie stirred. Awake now, he looked up to a clear blue sky. For a few moments Charlie tried to recall what had happened. Slowly it all came back to him. He had been in Lilliput but now, where was he? He remembered he had tumbled through water and landed here. But now his clothes were completely dry. He realised he must have slept for a while.

Charlie felt around. The surface below him was hard. He scraped away at it but it was heavily overgrown.

The surface did not seem to have any soil but was just a golden brick. Charlie excitingly scraped around to uncover more and more of the golden ground. No, Charlie thought, it isn't golden but yellow; it was definitely yellow. By this time, he was kneeling down as he continued to scrape the ground. With a cry of excitement, he jumped up and looked around. He realised he was in fact standing on a yellow brick road. 'Could this be Oz?' he wondered!

As he looked around the area, it was so overgrown he could not see anything but tree tops and blue sky, which was slowly turning slightly darker as the night started to draw in. He did not know what to do or where to go. Eventually he decided he should move forward to try and find some opening. He was excited but also a little anxious as he had no idea where he was or what was out there.

Charlie stumbled his way forward, getting entangled in all the weeds and the willow, which seemed constantly to get wrapped around his ankles, causing him to fall several times.

Slowly darkness closed in, and Charlie found it increasingly difficult to make out if he was going in a straight line or just round in circles. He stopped to try and find a focal point. Standing on his tiptoes, he was relieved to see a slight glimmer in the distance. With raised hopes on this sign of improvement in his fortunes, Charlie realised it was a light. With renewed enthusiasm, he set off in the direction of the light. He stopped every few steps to ensure he was keeping up his fight against the undergrowth as he approached his newfound friend, the light in the distance.

The whole place was so overgrown, Charlie was struggling to make any headway. At times the weeds, nettles and willow were so high he was unable to see over the top. From time to time, he would stop for a rest when he reached a tree. He leaned against it, partly to hold himself up and partly to use it to hide from anything that might be lurking out there.

Several times he thought he heard something. He stopped and listened but it was just his imagination running away with him, believing he could see shadows and objects in the darkened trees.

He kept a watchful eye in the distance for the glimmering light, which slowly and surely was beginning to become brighter.

He found it quite tiring, trying to wade through the solid mass of greenery. Charlie thought to himself how much easier it would have been if he'd had a torch and a big knife, or even a sword.

Suddenly, without any warning the undergrowth had gone. Yes, the grass was still overgrown in places, but on the whole as far as Charlie could see given his poor vision in the darkness it seemed to be completely clear. His journey towards the distant light now became a whole lot easier. But he still had the feeling he was being watched.

Eventually he found himself on the yellow brick road once again. He could see it clearly, damaged in places, but a road nonetheless. This made the journey easier and quicker and slowly the distant noises seemed to fade.

At last the light appeared to be within his grasp. As he approached, it became clear it was not one single light but lights from several places. Yes, the lights came from a very small village.

As he approached the village, he noticed a small cottage on its own slightly off the beaten track; it was closer to him than the village was. Charlie decided to move towards the light of the cottage and hoped he would be received favourably.

Charlie noticed that several lights were on in the cottage and it looked like a fire was lit because even in the dark Charlie could see smoke coming from the chimney.

He approached the cottage cautiously, looking carefully around for any hints of danger or any clues to where he might be.

With the light from the cottage he could see a number of logs waiting to be cut whilst several had been cut, chopped and stacked against the wall. Behind the logs lying on the ground he observed a wooden horse for cutting the logs, which still had a long piece of log on it. To the left was a shed with what looked like a small bench. Yes, it was a sitting bench with an axe resting against it.

The moon slipped behind the clouds again, leaving only the light from the cottage on the garden. From this distance Charlie tried to see if there was any movement within the cottage, as the curtains were open, but apart from a flickering glow from what must have been the fire, there was nothing to be seen.

Then without any warning the front door opened and a shaky voice shouted out: ‘Who goes there?’ There was a pause before the voice continued: ‘I’ll have no nonsense here. Show yourself.’

At first Charlie was frozen to the spot, but then he observed the person standing in the doorway. Charlie felt relieved and ecstatic at the same time. He had to take a second glance, but without a doubt it was Tin Man from Oz. Of course, the yellow brick road, and now Tin Man. There was no mistaking - it was Oz.

'Hello,' said Charlie.

'Come into the light so I can see you,' Tin Man instructed.

Tin Man moved slightly to let more light shine out of the cottage onto the garden.

'I am Charlie,' Charlie explained.

'I don't know anyone named Charlie,' Tin Man replied. 'Charlie, you said! Come closer so I can see you,' demanded Tin Man.

Charlie duly did as he was told. He was nearly right up at the front door when Tin Man spoke again.

'You are just a young lad,' Tin Man observed, with what seemed to be a smile.

'What are you doing wandering about so early in the morning?' he enquired.

'Look at the state of you!' tut-ting at the sight that stood before him.

Charlie took the opportunity to look at himself a little. True enough he was a sight. His trousers were torn and thick with greenery and mud. His hands were all scratched and bloody.

'Come in, come in and make yourself at home,' said Tin Man.

Charlie was delighted to be invited into the cottage, and took no time to think about it before entering.

The cottage was quite sparse in terms of furniture and objects. But it was lovely and warm. Charlie suddenly became aware of how cold he was and he made his way towards the fire to warm himself.

'Sit down, before you fall down,' pointed out Tin Man.

Charlie did as he was told and settled into the chair, enjoying the heat from the fire.

'Hot drink?' Tin Man offered. 'I don't have any food. Maybe there are some cookies left.' He scurried off into the kitchen.

Charlie settled down, happy to feel at ease. It was only then he realised how unsettled he had been. His eyes were getting heavy as the warmth of the fire made him sleepy.

'Here we go.' Tin Man returned with a cup of hot chocolate and several broken biscuits.

'What brings you here in the state you are in?' he asked again.

'It's a long story.' Charlie answered. He continued: 'I came through the undergrowth down there.' He did not want to share the story of coming from Lilliput.

'Oh, my word!' Tin Man exclaimed with a slight sense of fear in his voice. 'It is very overgrown. It hasn't always been that way,' he pointed out in a serious tone.

'Oh, my word, through that entire wilderness, how and why? He sighed as he put his tin hands on his hips. 'No, it has not always been like that. Such a shame.'

'Drink up lad, drink up. Funny how things change,' he continued.

Just then there was a knock at the door. Tin Man made his way to the door and opened it.

'You ok?' a voice asked sternly and somewhat shakily as if expecting trouble.

'Has it gone? Did you see it?' the voice enquired.

Tin Man was doing his best to calm the visitor down. Eventually Tin Man grabbed the man by the arm and pulled him into the cottage.

The man appeared in the light. The first thing Charlie saw was a large wooden stick with a club end. Then instantly Charlie smiled hugely and greeted the man: 'Hello.'

'This is what I was worried about. No problem in the end, but glad you came right over,' Tin Man explained.

The man looked at Charlie with his big bright eyes and smiled back.

'Meet Mr. Scarecrow.' Tin Man smiled pointing to the scarecrow. The scarecrow moved towards Charlie. He was about to offer his hand in friendship when he realised he had moved his club forward. Charlie sat back abruptly.

'Sorry, sorry,' Scarecrow said, dropping his club and offering his straw hand for Charlie to shake it.

Charlie was so excited about yet another memory from a story being unfolded in front of him.

Scarecrow and Tin Man were such fun. Not that they meant to be, but just in how they interacted with each other. One would start a sentence and the other would finish it; one would say something and the other would correct it. Charlie thought the whole situation was so welcoming and relaxing after such a fearful time in the forest.

Charlie was so desperate to say how he knew them from the story he had read, but never did as he didn't want to spoil the moment. They made such a fuss over Charlie it just seemed such a wonderful and peaceful time with these two characters.

'Another biscuit,' said Tin Man

'Tea,' said Scarecrow.

'Stop fussing,' Tin Man admonished him.

'But Charlie looks like he could do with more tea.' Scarecrow explained.

'Tea?' questioned Tin Man.

'Now who's fussing!' Scarecrow argued before bursting out laughing, which in turn made Charlie and Tin Man also laugh loudly. Charlie had not had as much fun for ages; he didn't want it to end. However, by mid-day he drifted off to sleep, as he was exhausted.

It was about 4PM when Charlie awoke. There was no sign of either Tin Man or Scarecrow. He got up from his chair and noticed the fire was still burning away with fresh logs. They couldn't be far away.

He went out the front door and sure enough there was Tin Man sitting on the bench enjoying the fresh air. As he turned and saw Charlie, he leaped up and moved in Charlie's direction.

'You are awake,' Tin Man stated.
'Charlie's awake,' he shouted towards the rear of the cottage. All of a sudden Scarecrow bounded round the corner with a big smile on his face, nearly pushing Tin Man out of the way to see Charlie.

'How are you, me boy?' Scarecrow asked. 'I thought you were dead!' he exclaimed. 'But I remembered humans need to sleep!!'

'That's only because I reminded you, you straw brain,' countered Tin Man. They all laughed.

'Are you ok?' enquired Tin Man. 'You look peaky!' he continued.

'Mmm,' answered Charlie. 'I'm hungry,' he added.

'Charlie's hungry,' Scarecrow repeated.

'I know I heard,' said Tin Man.

'Well, don't just stand there. Get him something to eat,' Scarecrow ordered. Tin Man looked at Scarecrow and gave him a funny look. He scratched his head and looked at Charlie before calling out in a loud voice.

'Charlie's hungry. We need to go to the village to get some food.'

‘Food, food?’ Scarecrow questioned.

‘Yes, well all I need is oil, grease and WD40 to keep me going. And you Mr Straw Head need only straw but Charlie needs more than that!’ He looked at Charlie before continuing: ‘I am right, ain’t I?’ Tin Man asked. Charlie laughed and they all laughed together. The next thing he knew they all joined hands together and marched down the road towards the village. Charlie was so excited before he knew it, he had started to hum the tune for ‘Follow the yellow brick road’, and without warning both Tin Man and Scarecrow in full voice were blasting the words out to the tune. They all went along merrily to the village, laughing, singing and above all, having such a good time together. Charlie found them both to be such good company.

Eventually they reached the village, which was bursting with activity.

‘Morning,’ Tin Man said to several people.

‘It’s afternoon, you silly clog,’ pointed out Scarecrow.

‘Just being polite!’ Tin Man replied

‘Pooolite,’ Scarecrow repeated, making fun of his friend as he stood there in front of him with hands on his bent knees. He lifted his left hand up with his pinkie aloft: ‘Politeee!’

Everyone laughed and even some of the people from the village joined in.

‘Who is your friend?’ a lady questioned. Both Scarecrow and Tin Man tried with full thrust to move forward to give an answer only to end up bumping into each other, and then fall about laughing. Charlie also laughing stepped over them and moved towards the lady.

'My name is Charl...'

'Charlie,' interrupted Scarecrow. 'His name is Charlie,' he reaffirmed as he took off his hat and bowed while pointing to Charlie.

'Hello, Charlie,' greeted the lady. She was in her mid-thirties and was carrying an old wicker basket full of vegetables and a loaf of bread.

'Well, Charlie,' she continued.

'How did you managed to get caught up with these two?' she asked laughing. It was clear to Charlie that this was a very close-knit and friendly village, with Scarecrow and Tin Man very much accepted by the village people even if they were viewed as the village idiots. From their antics, this would be true. You could not help loving such a couple of misfits. They melted everyone's heart with their actions and banter.

'I was just passing by,' Charlie explained, not wanting to say too much.

'You look quite ravenous,' she observed. 'Come, I will make you something to eat, whilst these two fix themselves out'.

Charlie went off with the lady in the direction of what seemed like a local café. It turned out that she was indeed the owner of the village café. 'The Warm House' it was called, and warm it was. Charlie sat down and enjoyed a hot bowl of soup and a large piece of crusty bread before being given a plate of chocolate ice cream. This was heaven, Charlie thought. Scarecrow and Tin Man didn't enter the café but stayed outside talking and sitting around waiting for Charlie to finish.

After Charlie had finished, he went in search of the lady, whose name he had learned was Penelope. 'Thank you so much for such a lovely meal,' he said, apologising for not being able to pay for it because he had no money.

'It's on the house,' she said before continuing: 'Anyone who can bring the spring back into those two is more than welcome.' She laughed as she looked at the window. Charlie turned round to see both Scarecrow and Tin Man peering in the window looking for him as he had moved away from the window. As he was out of sight, they went to see where he was.

'What a pair,' Penelope said. 'Such a shame they have been so down.' She frowned.

'How, why?' asked Charlie.

'It's a long story,' she replied. Scarecrow and Tin man were waving franticly from outside the window.

'Go, be off with you, young Charlie,' Penelope urged him. Charlie made his way towards the doorway before turning round and saying thank you for his food. Once in the street, the three hobbled off towards the cottage. They had only gone a few yards when Scarecrow started singing: 'follow the yellow brick road, follow the yellow brick road.' Charlie sang along with them both when suddenly Tin Man stopped.

'Where did you learn the song, to sing it so well?' he enquired. Charlie was taken by surprise and tried to find a quick answer by saying:

'My Dad taught me. He must have learned it from the village,' Charlie said hoping it would be a sufficient response to the question.

'Well, he taught you well,' Scarecrow answered, before bursting into song once again. The three set out with great gusto back on the road to the village.

When they arrived back at the cottage still singing, Tin Man stopped and looked towards the forest. Charlie was surprised by the sudden change of attitude.

'Everything alright?' asked Charlie.

'Yes, yes, don't mind him, the old sentimental thing that he is,' replied Scarecrow.

'What about?' asked Charlie.

'It's a long story,' said Tin Man, shrugging his shoulders and turning to look towards Charlie and Scarecrow.

'What shall we do now?' asked Scarecrow. Charlie decided not to leave it there, as it was clear they were hiding something.

'The lady at the café mentioned that something had happened in the past that made you both sad,' said Charlie.

‘It’s nothing,’ they answered in unison.

‘Nothing to do with your old friend, the lion?’ asked Charlie.

‘How do you know Lion?’ Scarecrow was startled.

‘Who told you?’ snarled Tin Man.

‘Better left alone,’ Scarecrow added.

‘Sorry I was only concerned for you both. ‘Charlie said with sadness in his voice.

‘Sit down,’ ordered Scarecrow and we will tell you a story. Scarecrow told Charlie the story of Dorothy and their journey to Oz to see the wizard. Charlie was quite excited. Here he was being told the story by the very characters in the story. ‘How unreal is that?’ he thought. Occasionally Tin Man would butt in to put his spin on the tale. They related the story right up to the point where Dorothy left in the magic hot air balloon. Such a wonderful experience.

‘Sad day, but wonderful at the same time,’ observed Tin Man. Scarecrow continued: ‘We three were all so happy. I had my brain, Tin Man had his heart and Lion had his courage. All was well for a while but then it all went wrong. Yes, we were sad Dorothy left, but we still had each other until that sad day. Scarecrow stopped and looked up to the sky and then down at the ground, shaking his head. There was a silence for a few moments, and Charlie could wait no more.

‘What happened?’ Charlie enquired.

'No, no, enough is enough,' said Scarecrow. Charlie felt he didn't want to leave it there, so he pushed.

'We are all friends here,' he pointed out in a serious tone.

'What happened?' he asked again. Scarecrow shook his head gesturing with his hands to indicate he was not going to say.

'Lion lost it,' blurted out Tin Man.

'Shh,' Scarecrow cautioned. 'The boy doesn't need to hear it.'

'I, I only tried...' Tin Man responded before being interrupted by Charlie.

'Yes, I do,' Charlie pleaded. 'Please continue.'. Scarecrow put his hands on Tin Man's shoulders as he looked away before continuing.

'Lion attacked a little boy,' he sobbed. 'He didn't hurt him, but the village folk cast him out.'

'Yes, but he had been naughty up to that point,' Tin Man added.

Scarecrow turned to him: 'That is true. He sort of became a nuisance around the place, pushing his weight about.' Tin Man then cut him off, saying: 'We tried to get him to stop, but he just said it was his courage making him do it!!' Now he sobbed too.

'Tragic, so tragic,' sobbed Tin Man.

'Stop that or you will just rust up again,' said Scarecrow.

'I can't help it.' Tin Man said.

'He was going about taking sweets from children, and scaring old people by roaring at them all the time.' Tin Man explained.

'It was so scary,' Scarecrow added.

'Sounds like a bully to me!' exclaimed Charlie.

'No, he was definitely a Lion, not a bull,' argued Tin Man.

'You might have a heart, but I often wonder if you have a brain,' scorned Scarecrow. 'He was meaning he was acting like a bully, not that he was a bull, silly,' he explained.

'Don't you call me silly?' stated Tin Man in a somewhat angry tone as he stepped forward.

'Stop, stop!' Charlie shouted. 'It is Lion we are talking about. Scarecrow didn't mean to call you silly! Did you?' Charlie said looking at Scarecrow.

'No, no of course not. He is my best friend and I don't want to hurt him.' He put his hands on his hips.

'But sometimes he can just knock the stuffing out of you.' They all laughed. After a minute or two Charlie asked: 'Where is lion now?'

Scarecrow turned and pointed to the forest. 'In there,' he stated.

'Nobody can go near the place now as he terrorises them.' He shuddered as Tin Man continued the story.

'When he was chased out of the village, he took to staying in the forest, but ever since then no one - no one has been able to enter the forest without being terrorised. Nobody has ever been injured, but everyone is scared to enter. I am surprised you survived the forest, without encountering trouble,' observed Tin Man.

'Umm.' Charlie thought for a moment and then stood up and said: 'There was something in the forest following me.'

Both Scarecrow and Tin Man gasped as Charlie continued: 'But I don't think he would have attacked me!' he said defiantly.

'Why?' Both Tin Man and Scarecrow questioned together.

Charlie went on: 'Because he didn't know what I would do!' He laughed.

'I think he is a bully and isn't courageous at all,' he stated. 'In my school we had a bully. He used to pick on me, but my Dad told me to stand up to him.' He stood there in a proud posture with arms on hips. Scarecrow looked intently and asked what happened.

Charlie continued: 'Well ...' Then he paused as both Scarecrow and Tin Man listened closely.

'One day he came at me. It was really scary! I was shaking in my boots, but remembering what my Dad said, I stood and looked at him right in the eye and said, 'really.' Charlie smiled.

'What happened, what happened!!? ?' Scarecrow questioned earnestly.

Charlie laughed: 'Nothing, just nothing. He turned and walked away and I never had any more trouble with him.' He stood tall trying to show how clever he was, before continuing: 'You see, standing up to a bully is the only way to put them in their place. I think this is what has happened to Lion, and he has no idea how to change until someone stands up to him.' Charlie concluded, rubbing his chin.

He walked over and sat on the bench in front of the shed. Tin Man and Scarecrow were fooling around. One was pretending to be the bully and the other saying "really". They were having a great time. Charlie sat quietly on the bench, and then without warning he got up and shouted: 'Scarecrow, get your club. Tin Man, get a stick. We're off to the forest.' Charlie was so serious, both were shocked.

'Forest?' they both exclaimed.

'Yes,' Charlie confirmed. 'This has gone on long enough. We have to put an end to it.' Charlie turned and headed to the forest.

'Wait, wait,' they both shouted.

'It's too dangerous,' Tin Man gestured holding his hands up to his eyes.

'Nonsense. Let's go.' Charlie turned back and looked at them.

'Scarecrow, your club. Tin Man, a long stick and follow me,' he ordered. Both Scarecrow and Tin Man did as they were told and made their way along the road with Charlie.

'Follow the yellow brick road, follow the yellow brick road,' Charlie sang in order to give them courage to soldier on. Before long the three of them were singing in full voice and dancing as they set off towards the forest. They were having a fun time laughing and joking, but well below all this hilarity the three were nervous. After all, what would happen in the forest?

Before long the three intrepid warriors could see the start of the forest. At approximately two hundred yards from the forest, Charlie stopped. Tin Man and Scarecrow had by this time intentionally fallen a few steps behind him. The three stood there for a moment, looking intently at the shadowy trees and the encounter that loomed ahead for them.

Charlie was the first to speak. He turned around and was quite surprised at how far behind him the two had taken their stance.

'Come on, lads. We are in this together,' he shouted.

'Yes, together,' they both responded, not sounding at all convinced.

'Here's the plan,' Charlie stated.

'We have a plan?' asked Scarecrow.

'Of course, we have a plan,' Charlie replied. 'I just haven't thought of it yet. Any ideas?' he continued, scratching his head.

'Tea,' suggested Tin Man. 'We can go home and have tea.'

'No. We have come here to put an end to this nonsense and an end it must be.' Charlie retorted.

'End to whom?' Scarecrow questioned.

‘The best thing we can do is go to the start of the forest and ask Lion to come out and talk,’ Charlie said hoping for some kind of reaction.

‘A truce,’ stated Scarecrow.

‘Great! What an idea!’ responded Charlie. Scarecrow stood up straight looking rather pleased with himself.

‘See that,’ Scarecrow said to Tin Man. ‘A great idea.’ He proudly announced grinning with all the might he could muster in Tin Man’s direction. Tin Man was not convinced. He smirked slightly while trying his best to come up with another great idea.

‘I know,’ he proposed. ‘We can go home and forget all about it. It is about time I oiled my arms and legs.

I’m off, see you later!’ He was about to turn around and walk away when Charlie grabbed him by the arm.

‘We are all in this together,’ Charlie pointed out. ‘After all, Lion was a friend was he not?’ Both Tin Man and Scarecrow nodded their heads simultaneously.

‘Well then, we owe it to that friendship to try and make him see the error of his ways, do we not?’ Charlie questioned, not really knowing if what he said made real sense, but it was meant to get them back together.

‘Yes,’ consented Scarecrow.

'Indeed,' agreed Tin Man. 'And I think when we come up with a good plan we could come back and put it into action.'
Scarecrow nodded with approval. Charlie was slightly exasperated. 'Come on, lads, pull together. We are the three musketeers. One for all and all for one.'

'The three what?' Scarecrow asked.

'The three... never, mind that ,we are all together,' Charlie responded. 'All we want to do is ask Lion to come out and talk, that's all. After all what could go wrong?'

'Ask him out for a cup of tea and a Scarecrow, Tin Man and Boy to eat,' observed Tin Man.

Charlie was beginning to get frustrated with their lack of belief in what they were doing. He was just about to get angry with them both when Scarecrow spoke.

'One for all and all for one,' he said. 'We were all for one before with Dorothy, surely that means something.' Scarecrow stated. It seemed the mood had now changed. Scarecrow walked over and stood beside Charlie.

'I for one am ready to be one for all, come and join with us, Tin Man,' Scarecrow beckoned. Tin Man was not convinced, but at the same time he knew that Scarecrow and he had been friends for a long time, and he did not want anything to bring an end to that. Slowly but surely Tin Man raised his head.

'What was that? One for one and all for whatever it was.' He tried to repeat the words

Scarecrow had said but just mumbled as he marched across and stood beside Charlie.

'We are the three mustard men,' Tin Man proudly stated.

'Musketeers,' Charlie corrected.

'I have no idea who they are or how you say it,' announced Scarecrow. 'But we are all together as one, I think.' He looked questioningly at Charlie.

'Great, now we are getting somewhere,' Charlie replied confidently.

'I think we will walk slowly,' as Charlie started to speak, he was interrupted by Tin Man. 'Very slowly,' he said.

Charlie sniggered and continued: 'As I was saying, I think we go to the edge of the wood and shout for Lion to come and say hello and have a chat for old time's sake.' He paused. 'What do you think?' He looked at his two colleagues hoping for some reaction, but there was none. Scarecrow looked at Tin Man and Tin Man looked at Scarecrow and then they both looked at Charlie.

'Could we just not sneak up on him and knock him on the head, tie him up and do something with him?' Tin Man asked very nervously.

'No, we want to give him a chance to be friends,' Charlie advised. Charlie turned around and looked towards the woods. Scarecrow and Tin Man also turned and looked in the same direction.

'You first, Charlie, you are the leader,' Tin Man proudly announced.

'Since when did I become the leader?' Charlie questioned. 'All for one and one for all, we said.'

'Yes, we both agree,' added Scarecrow.

'And we are both behind you,' shared Tin Man. Charlie looked at them both and decided it was no use just standing here waiting. He knew before long they would both end up getting scared and going home. Charlie decided it would be better if he moved forward and allowed them to follow him. Charlie took the first few steps and looked back at the two, who seemed to be rooted to the spot.

'Come on, you two! All for one and one for all,' he repeated.

'Yea, yea. All for all and one for one,' Tin Man responded not quite getting the hang of the phrase. The two moved forward to catch up with Charlie, who smiled nervously, turned and moved towards the forest. After a few steps Charlie stopped to check where the two were. To his surprise he nearly knocked them down when he turned around. Scarecrow got a fright with the sudden change in Charlie's movements.

'Sorry,' Charlie apologised. Charlie's voice was close to a whisper.

'Not far now. Scarecrow, you have your club, and Tin Man, you have your stick. Good. We hopefully shouldn't need to use them, but just in case be ready.' Charlie tried to be reassuring in his instructions. Both Tin

Man and Scarecrow nodded in agreement, but at the same time looked terrified.

'It would be better if one of you called to Lion as he knows your voice. I might frighten him off and make him angry.' Charlie suggested. Both Scarecrow and Tin Man stated at the same time;

'He can do it.'

'You were closer to him than I was,' pointed out Tin Man.

'No, you spent more time with him than I did.' They both argued.

'Shh,' commanded Charlie.

'Look, all you have to do is one of you, or both of you, shout out and ask Lion to come and say hi. It can't be any easier.' Charlie was not totally convinced despite this statement, but he hoped that one of them would take the responsibility upon himself.

'Okay,' agreed Tin Man. 'I will shout to him.' He looked at Scarecrow hoping that he would offer, but no offer was made. Charlie smiled at him and indicated that they should move forward a little more so that when they shouted Lion, he would hear. After moving forward about another ten paces or so, Charlie stopped and raised his hand as if he was guiding an army assault on the enemies' camp.

'Okay, Tin Man. Call to him,' he ordered.

'Oh, Lion,' Tin Man said, more as a whimper than indicating an invitation.

'Louder than that Tin Man. You want him to hear you and know we mean business,' Charlie explained before offering some encouraging words.

'You can do it, all for one and ... .' He was interrupted by Scarecrow who continued: 'And one for all.'

'Ok, I know that,' Tin Man stated. He cleared his throat, stood up straight and shouted:

'Lion, oh Mr Lion, are you there?' he questioned. The three stood there silently for what seemed ages but in truth it was only a few seconds.

'Auch, well then,' said Scarecrow. 'He isn't there. We will just need to come back another time,' he said hoping that the others would take up his statement and they would indeed go home.

'Try again,' said Charlie. Tin Man looked more nervous this time, so Charlie patted him on the shoulder and said, 'It is okay. I will do it.' Charlie turned, cleared his throat and shouted: 'Hello, Mr Lion. Are you there?' Charlie looked intently but nothing seemed to happen. He turned and faced Scarecrow and Tin Man with a blank expression not knowing what he could do next. Both Tin Man and Scarecrow looked back at him in amusement, but within a few seconds their expressions changed into one of fear. Charlie sensed that something must be happening behind him so he slowly turned around. He was very nervous now, and he felt butterflies swelling up in his stomach. As Charlie turned, he felt Tin Man and Scarecrow scurry in behind him, looking to hide from what may happen. As they stared into the forest, all they could see was a patch of grass moving like a wave from side to side, slowly and surely making its way forward towards them. They stood frozen to the spot. They were all too petrified to say or do anything, never mind move. Eventually the wave of grass got closer until eventually it was only a few feet to the end of the wood and undergrowth. The wave seemed to stop. They all stared, waiting, watching for what seemed a lifetime. When nothing happened, Tin Man whispered: 'Maybe he isn't here!'

Then suddenly, without any warning a head popped above the waving grass. Both Tin Man and Scarecrow jumped, making Charlie jump too with fright. It was Lion right enough, with his eyes staring straight at the waiting, shivering, frightened group.

'Who are you?' Lion roared with clear sounds of discontent and anger in his voice. In a squeaky and frightened voice, Tin Man said: 'It's me, Tin Man and Scarecrow! You're f-friends!' It came out in a splutter and somewhat in desperation rather than a statement. Lion shook his head. His mane waved triumphantly in the air as he gave off a sense of superiority.

'I know who you are. You rust bucket and your straw head idiot there!' he commented with a smirk as he tried to instil a sense of fear into the two frightened old friends. It was clear it was working because Charlie could feel the fear coming from them. They tightened their grip on him, hoping that in some way Charlie would protect them from this monster of a lion, which moved another step closer to them, showing off his strong muscular physique.

'I meant who is the pale-faced wimp of a boy you have with you?' He smirked and once again shook his head. He moved another step closer to intimidate the waiting posse in front of him.

'What do you mean by coming here and disturbing my forest and my peace and quiet?' he roared trying to put them all on the back foot. It seemed to work as Tin Man and Scarecrow tried to pull Charlie back with them to give a sense of retreat. Charlie stood still; not that he wasn't scared, he was terrified, but he knew that if he acted in the same way as the other two, Lion would have won and they would have run all the way back to the cottage in defeat.

'Wait a minute. I recognise you!' Lion roared as he reached out with his head towards Charlie.

'You were that scoundrel who clumsily forced his way through the forest a few days ago, making a real mess of the place.' He stopped to give a disapproving look at Charlie, which was designed to make him feel fearful, before he continued: 'Luckily for you, you had left the forest before I could find out who was causing all the commotion.'

He stopped waiting for a reaction. Charlie at first felt himself weakening and the hair on the back of his neck was standing on end. Sweat was beginning to build up on his palms and his forehead. But then a thought came to Charlie. I stopped several times for a rest and at one stage I fell asleep for a while. It was not as if I was only in the forest for a few minutes. I was in there for ages. He had plenty of time to do something! This seemed to give him a little courage. Clearing his throat and clenching his right fist, he responded: 'So what about it?' Surprisingly it came out quite sternly and firmly, which pleased him.

Tin Man shook him saying quietly in his ear: 'Don't make him any angrier.' Tin Man was shaking like a leaf, causing some of his tin to rattle. Scarecrow was not much different. His heavy breathing and whimpering were very unsettling; but surprising to Charlie his two colleagues stood close beside him. Charlie tried to give the impression of not being afraid and lifted his head and stuck his chest out in defiance even though he felt he was about to collapse. Lion responded angrily to the answer and roared before looking towards the cowering threesome, wondering what to do. Charlie again cleared his throat and decided to challenge Lion's comments a little.

'Your forest, who said it was your forest?' He paused for a second as Lion was becoming more agitated. Tin Man froze and Scarecrow gave a little squeak as if to say something. They were not happy that the situation seemed to make Lion angry and unsettled them more, but in true one for one and one for all, they managed to stay close and, in some ways, uncomfortably close, Charlie thought.

'Surely the forest belongs to everyone and not just one bully of a Lion,' Charlie argued trying to sound triumphant. Scarecrow gave a little whimper as he shook severely. Tin Man tried to pull away but Charlie grabbed his arm and pulled him back.

'You are nothing but a bully,' Charlie retorted. Lion was enraged. The anger building up within him was clear to see. He scratched his left paw on the ground. Tin Man was shaking; Scarecrow was whimpering loudly.

'A bully and nothing but a bully my Dad would say,' Charlie continued, trying to provoke the lion into action. He turned and whispered to Scarecrow and Tin Man: 'Ready with your stick and club in case we need it.' Tin Man moved his stick out to the side trying to show Charlie he still had it. Scarecrow lifted the club above his head, lowering it in front of Charlie more in hope that he would take it, but Charlie didn't. Then it happened. Lion roared with all his might and leaped out towards Charlie. Scarecrow cringed and held his stick out in front. Tin Man let go of Charlie and was about to run, but Charlie gripped tightly to Tin Man's arm not letting him go. This was more from fear rather than preventing him from leaving. Lion now was in full flight heading towards Charlie, shouting at the top of his voice.

'MY FOREST!' At that moment Charlie could feel the spittle from Lion as he roared. All the hairs on his body stood on end with fright. He was shaking all over but he stood firm. Just as Lion's face became level with Charlie's, he prepared to roar again. Charlie ducked out of the way and pushed his two friends clear shouting: It's now or never. Charlie turned and saw the eyes of Lion staring straight at him. Instinctively he lifted his hand and slapped the Lion straight along his wet angry nose. It all seemed to happen in slow motion, but Charlie made a firm connection with the side of Lion's nose. Lion dropped to the ground without much of an effort. Both Scarecrow and Tin Man noticed a slight change in Lion as if he had been taken by surprise by Charlie's action and they went forward towards Lion with their club and stick outright, looking to protect Charlie rather than aiming to hurt Lion. Charlie moved towards Lion and put his foot on the back of his neck. He didn't know why but felt he had to. All of a sudden Lion burst into tears.

'Don't hurt me, don't hurt me. I was only joking,' he whimpered trying to move his two front paws over his face to protect himself. Scarecrow and Tin Man looked at each other in bewilderment. Charlie turned and looked at them both and gave a small smile.

'Why shouldn't we?' Charlie shouted at Lion. Winking at Scarecrow, he went on: 'Scarecrow, use your club!' At the same time, he waved to Scarecrow to indicate to him not to use his club. This confused Scarecrow a little but he knew he wasn't to hit Lion. Lion whimpered.

'No, no. Please don't hurt me,' he pleaded as he tried to curl up to protect himself.

Charlie laughed softly: 'Told you he was a coward and a bully.'

Both Scarecrow and Tin Man lifted their hands in triumphant celebration. Charlie still had his foot on Lion, on the back of his neck as he wanted to make sure Lion wouldn't take him by surprise.

'What shall we do with him?' asked Charlie, trying to sound firm and in charge, although by this time he was beginning to shake a little as the whole situation had been quite an ordeal. Tin Man and Scarecrow looked at Charlie blankly not knowing what to say, but both were delighted that all had gone well and that they had survived.

It was then Scarecrow had a thought: 'Maybe we should slap him in chains and throw the key away!' He was jesting as he knew Charlie was looking only to put pressure on Lion to accept his defeat fully.

'Not a bad idea,' remarked Charlie looking at Tin Man whilst smiling. Lion whimpered, clearly disapproving of the suggestion.

'Tie him up and put him on display in the town so all the people will get their revenge on the terror he has inflicted,' Tin Man announced triumphantly, joining in the victory celebrations. Lion lay there shaking and whimpering.

'No, no. Please no!' Lion whispered.

'What was that you said?' asked Charlie.

'Please no, no! All my courage is gone. I am not the Lion I was honestly,' Lion pleaded.

'That was not courage,' Charlie replied. 'That was just down-right bullying, scaring people like that.' He leaned down to ensure Lion heard him.

'Please don't hurt me. I didn't mean it,' Lion sobbed.

'It was horrible in the forest, so lonely and dark!' Sob. 'No one to talk to, no friends.' He was sobbing uncontrollably now. Charlie lifted his foot off the back of Lion's neck, but Lion remained curled up in a protective ball whimpering and shaking.

'Come on, you old lump of fur,' commanded Tin Man. Charlie smiled at Scarecrow, who fidgeted and moved towards Lion. He bent down quite timidly, still afraid of what might happen.

'Still want friends like us?' whispered Scarecrow, not sure if he was doing the right thing coming so close to Lion.

'I wish,' sobbed Lion. 'I have been so horrible and nasty.' He gave a large groan and pulled his paws over his head.

'Come on, old friend,' said Tin Man soothingly. Lion stirred and looked towards Tin Man.

'We can still be friends after all that I have done?' he whimpered wiping a tear and his nose at the same time.

'As long as you don't start that old bullying again,' replied Charlie. Lion looked at Charlie and gave a wry smile.

'Nasty right hook you have for such a small boy!' He sniggered at Charlie and Charlie punched the air in fun and they all laughed.

Lion rose to his feet and Scarecrow and Tin Man walked over towards him. The tension had gone and it was clear Lion, Tin Man and Scarecrow all wanted bygones to be bygones.

'Come on,' said Charlie. 'I am hungry. Can we go and get a bite to eat?

'Certainly,' replied Tin Man. 'Cookies all round,' he stated triumphantly. The four set off down the road.

'What was that song you were singing as you approached?' Lion questioned, more in the hope of a singsong than anything else, which truly happened as Scarecrow and Tin Man burst into joyful singing: 'Follow the yellow brick road'.

Back at the cottage after they had eaten all the cookies and had tea, Charlie had a question.

'We are going to have to tell the villagers the forest is safe and that Lion is sorry for all he did.' Scratching his head, he tried to provoke them all into a discussion on what would happen next. The group sat discussing solutions late into the night. Lion was more terrified of going near the village. But in the end, it was agreed that, in the morning, Lion, along with his two friends, Tin Man and Scarecrow, and their new friend, Charlie, would go to the village where Lion would apologise to the villagers and ask for their forgiveness.

He would ask to be able to stay locally, but if they asked him to leave, they would all move somewhere else together.

The next morning the four friends awoke. There was a bit of tension in the air, not with each other, but with the thought of the coming challenge. Charlie broke the silence.

'I think I will go to the village and invite them to come to the village green where you all can be standing' he instructed. They all looked at him wondering where this was going.

'I will invite them to come and listen and observe Lion's pledge of friendship.' Charlie wasn't confident in his suggestion, or if it would work. But it was clear something had to be said for things to move on. Eventually they all pulled themselves together and set off for the village.

As they approached the village, nerves began to set in. Lion wanted to go back. He was clearly shaking. His two friends patted him on the back.

'Come on, old man,' encouraged Scarecrow. 'We are in this together.'

Surprisingly they all managed to get to the village green without incident and no one seemed to have noticed Lion at all. Charlie set off to round up one or two villagers. Eventually a crowd had gathered at the edge of the green. Lion had hidden himself slightly behind a tree, not really wanting to face the people he had scared all this time, not to mention inconvenienced -- whilst he had closed off the forest road, the villagers had to make a couple of detours to avoid the forest.

Charlie stood in front of the villagers. He was very nervous and not sure what to say or do. Scarecrow and Tin Man stood slightly behind him.

'Yesterday,' Charlie shouted. This drew the people's attention to him. 'We three friends went to the forest.' He was interrupted by a little sigh from the crowd as they realised the danger.

'We called a truce with Lion and he apologised for all his wrongdoing and wanted to ask you all to forgive him.' The crowd was silent and no one moved. Charlie realised he had to go on. 'Lion has come here today to ask if you can forgive him!' He paused whilst trying to think, before continuing: 'And he wants to know if you can help him fix the forest and re-open the yellow brick road.' He stopped and looked at the crowd. It was total silence until one old gentleman stepped forward scratching his head.

'Would this mean we could use the forest road again?' he enquired.

'Yes!' exclaimed Charlie. Just then Lion appeared from behind the tree. The crowd was shocked. Clearly, they had not seen Lion, even although it was quite obvious he was there behind the tree. The crowd stepped back gasping, shocked.

'Don't be afraid,' soothed Tin Man. 'He will not harm you; he never wanted to, it was all wind and hot air.' Tin Man looked at Lion. The crowd didn't know whether to believe him or not, but they remained there. Charlie stood, trying to reassure the crowd as Tin Man and Scarecrow encouraged Lion to move forward to speak.

'I am very, very sorry,' said Lion. 'I don't know what came over me. I wanted to be courageous and strong.' He shook his head in sadness. His head was bent low nearly touching the ground in shame. Everyone could see he was ashamed at what he had done, but they were still unsure of him.

'All I want to do is have my friends back!' He turned to face Tin Man and Scarecrow. They moved towards him. Scarecrow reached down and gave him a hug whilst Tin Man patted him on his head.

'It was so lonely, scary and dark in the forest. I didn't know what to do. How could you ever forgive me?' Lion sobbed quite uncontrollably. He looked at Charlie in the hope that Charlie would continue talking. But just at that moment without warning the old gentleman who had spoken earlier walked over and patted him on the head. He turned and looked at the crowd and said: 'I think I will help him fix the road!' He looked at the crowd. 'Who will help?' he asked. Several in the crowd offered to help whilst others raised their hands. Charlie stepped forward with a suggestion: 'How about we meet at this time tomorrow at Tin Man's cottage and arrange to re-open the road.' He tried to sound as enthusiastic as possible. The crowd cheered.

‘Tomorrow then,’ shouted Charlie triumphantly. The crowd responded by giving a cheer and slowly they all started to move off. Eventually it was only the old man and his grandson, Tin Man, Scarecrow, Charlie and Lion left on the green. The old man went over to Lion and looked at him straight in the eye.

‘Don’t let us down, son,’ he said sternly before setting off back towards the village. Lion looked up and watched the man and his grandson walk away.

‘I will not, sir, indeed not. You can count on me.’ For the first time this day Lion managed to give a small smile. He looked towards Tin Man, Scarecrow and Charlie and smiled gratefully.

‘Well, better be of,’ said Tin Man. ‘Got a lot to arrange.’

‘We sure have,’ agreed Scarecrow. Charlie did too, and they all set off towards the cottage. As they walked back towards the cottage, Scarecrow looked at Tin Man and asked: ‘What do we have to arrange?’ They all laughed at Scarecrow but he continued to look puzzled as they briskly made their way home.

It was a big day the next day. Both Charlie and Lion had had a restless night. Tin Man and Scarecrow didn’t seem to have a worry in the world. Scarecrow was the first to look out of the window.

‘Ah! No one’s coming,’ he mumbled.

‘Early yet,’ remarked Charlie as he took another bite of toast from the loaf he had got from the village the day before. Two minutes later, Scarecrow walked over to the window.

'Still no one!' he observed, shrugging his shoulders.

'Will you stop that!' called Lion. 'You are making me nervous,' he snarled.

'Stop what?' asked Scarecrow. Charlie laughed.

'Sit down. It's still early yet. It isn't even eight o'clock. We didn't go to the village until after ten yesterday and we did say this time tomorrow.' He took another bite of toast and a sip of tea. Scarecrow moved away from the window and sat at the table, putting his elbows on it and resting his head on his arms. The four sat round the table for a while discussing not only old times but also what they would do first at the forest. Scarecrow eventually got bored and rose towards the window.

'Come away from the window,' ordered Tin Man.

'Fellas, you better come and look at this,' Scarecrow cried, pointing at the window. Charlie rose from the table and made his way to the window, closely followed by Tin Man. Lion stayed at the table afraid to go and see; after all, what if it was bad news.

'Would you look at that!' chirped Charlie, looking back round at Lion.

'Wow!' exclaimed Tin Man. Scarecrow could hardly contain himself. Lion slowly rose from the table and walked towards the window. He was only a few feet away when Charlie moved to the side and then Lion could see that the whole village was standing waiting, looking intently at the cottage, waiting for the occupants in the cottage to come out. They all had spades, forks, wheelbarrows, everything they could possibly need to clear the road. Tin Man made his way towards the door.

'Come on, you lot. No time to waste.' With that Tin Man disappeared outside, followed by Scarecrow and Charlie. Lion was a little slower in going out. He was still a little nervous at what was about to happen. As Lion came through the door, everyone was looking at him. Charlie moved forward and said. 'Don't worry. Everything is all right.' He smiled and then stood up and clapped his hands. The whole crowd did the same thing. It was a real hero's welcome. Lion straightened up and marched outside the door smiling triumphantly at the people. He motioned a thank you to the entire crowd, and they stopped clapping and cheering. Lion walked to the front of them all, looked towards the forest and then back at the people.

'What are you all standing there for? We have a lot of work to do.' He waved to them all to follow him. Tin Man and Scarecrow ran up beside Lion, closely followed by the crowd. Charlie was slightly behind everyone. Then from the front of the crowd the sound of singing started. 'Follow the yellow brick road, follow the yellow brick road.' Charlie joined in; it was such a wonderful time.

The Morning After

'Charlie, Charlie!' came a sound in the distance.

'Are you coming down? Your breakfast is getting cold.' Sure enough Charlie could smell the bacon and eggs. I'm home, he thought. I'm home. He jumped out of bed, put on his dressing gown and ran down the stairs.

'Are you all right, Charlie?' asked his father.

'What are you smiling about?' enquired his mother. Charlie thought for a moment, looked at his mother and father and thought 'magic Niger seed!'

'Oh, nothing!' replied Charlie. 'Nothing at all,' he confirmed as he dipped a slice of bread into his fried egg.

Epilogue

Charlie has grown up. Now much, much older with children of his own, he often remembers the dream and the story of the magic Niger seed.

As he takes time to reflect on its teaching and his thoughts, he is aware of the importance of always having friends around, people who you can rely on and encourage through life. Friends no matter what order of rank or walk of life, they are always just that, friends. Friends you can share with, have an extended family with. All friends no matter where they are should never be taken for granted; we must always seek to value them and their worth throughout our life.

I think we all can learn from Charlie's dream.

And there is another thought, a secret.
Every now and then when he in his bed sleeping, Charlie often has a dream that his magic Niger seed takes him off back into one of his old stories which he remembers his Dad had told him. Often when he wakens, he wonders if, when he tells his children these same stories, they too will ever encounter this magical world.

Conclusion

This story of the magic Niger seed and Charlie drifting into the lives of fictional characters in his sleep has much to teach us.

Charlie's encounter with characters drawn from fiction shows us that in real life we too can drift in and out of people's lives in our own magical journey of life. It teaches us that no matter what we do or say we will and can influence people in their walk no matter if it is a chance encounter or a long life friendship.

The truth is no matter what we think of ourselves, we do all have input into other people's lives whether we want to or not. In Charlie's dream the main characters had an influence on the story as a whole. It involved past encounters as well as present ones. Although this story is of course fiction, it contains lessons for us to learn.

Some of our relationships may be hostile ones, difficult and strange ones as well as happy and caring ones. But no matter what relationships we have, we must try our best always to be loving and caring, remembering that we have no control over how other people act, but we do have control over how we act and what we say and do.

Often our response to a situation can either inflame, release tension or give a sense of hope and peace. But in all things we can never expect to change someone unless they first decide to change. We are not wholly responsible for their actions, but we are for ours. Being hostile because they are hostile doesn't mean it is right. It just means that you are easily influenced by your surroundings and not fully in control of your own actions. I have often heard it said that 'I told them what I thought; after all it is my right to have my say.' The truth is it isn't our right always to say what we think. Often it is all about just being heard. Often these replies do not help any situation or indeed help the person to change; but only to be more negative in their response.

No, I believe we are all called to be loving and kind to one another no matter the situation. To always have your say says more to your own ego than it does about your own self as a person.

I believe my faith in God gives me a chance to help create a character within me that allows the love of God, the creator of all, to help create the love and care which is needed in the world. A good positive attitude rather than the self-egotistical one is required to encourage people in the world today. Just because I am a person of faith, it doesn't mean I am a better person than anyone else; but it does give me a responsibility to try and create a good positive attitude in all I say and do.

I believe my faith allows me to be more self-controlled, caring and above all interested in showing people the true purpose in life, which is to show love to all God's creation.

Sometimes in life we come across people who no matter what you do, show or care for, they never change; they are always on the take, always looking for self and not willing to share. People like this are usually just takers, following their own egos for what they can get. We can only live in hope that we may influence them at some time in their life; we may have planted a seed within them to change. But it is maybe not our place to change them, but someone else's. Therefore, we should not feel bad if we try and move on and leave them to find their own path, to follow then on to the next venture in their life.

However, there are those we come across who accept the love, compassion we give and in response they show it in return, not just with you but with others. These people can encourage and strengthen us in our walk as we strengthen and encourage them in theirs.

It is the calling to all mankind to love, care, cherish all creation.

Jesus taught us that we must love our enemies and not just people who are nice to us. Even people who treat us badly can love their own kind.

He taught that we should live for each other and not just for self, ensuring that no matter what, wherever we go, we leave that place in a better position than when we first entered.

With that thought in mind, I pray that in life you may find true love, peace and happiness, and in whatever way possible, ensure that you leave peace and love wherever you may go.

God bless you.

The Garden of Peace and Sorrow. Eden

It was just another day in paradise; the sun shone, glittering off the river like twinkling stars shooting up from its flow. The response to the eye brought happiness and love to the heart and mind, which in turn matched the surroundings in this beautiful garden. The trees were as green and lush as always. The fruit trees invited a welcoming glance of abundance, whilst the flowers bloomed and danced to capture the warm sunlit rays. The birds tweeted in their usual chorus, harmonising in a beautiful symphony of song and joy.

The animals went about their daily business, content as always, totally free and safe from harm. As I said, it was just another day in paradise. But today, this day, something had just happened that was about to make everything change. Gone would be the peace and tranquillity, to be replaced with a heaviness of heart, taking paradise from a haven of peace to a place of sadness. A dark cloud loomed over the garden's beauty as guilt hung over us, wasting our soul away. It was no use. This cloud was unnatural for here. It conflicted with the creation of this place, and this cloud was created by me.

I sat hopeless and empty at the side of the river in contemplation. This was my favourite spot where I would always start my day. But today, this day, was so, so different; it was no normal day and no matter what I thought, there was nothing I could do to change the situation.

I had no idea what these feelings were as I had never experienced anything like this before. I had no explanation for why I felt so low and so poor! I had no way of comprehending how I felt or how my actions would affect my relationship with all of this creation, never mind with my master and friend. And little did I know how it would affect all humanity.

Suddenly a sound from behind me startled me from my deep inner thoughts.

'What are you doing sitting there?' It was my gifted partner from the Lord, Eve.

'You can't sit there all day feeling sorry for yourself!' she exclaimed.

I suppose that is what I was doing, but since I had never done this before, I had nothing to compare it with; after all I had never had a feeling such as this. Before this, everything was simple, clear and joyous, but now I didn't know what to think. There was no excitement, just emptiness. The sunshine may still be there, but a cloud hung over me.

'Coming!' I replied as I lifted myself from my peaceful shrine knowing that everything would never be the same. It could never return to the way it was.

I caught up with Eve in the cluster of the pomegranate trees.

'Hurry,' she said in an almost frantic voice.

'He will be here soon.' She continued pulling me towards her so that I would move faster. It was then realisation hit me: The Lord, our friend, always came to meet us for our morning walk together, but today, how could we face him?

'Come on, hurry,' she urged, somewhat nervously but almost in a whisper.

I sensed the urgency and we both ran towards the safety of the trees.

'We can't let him find us like this!' she continued, as we hid down behind some of the rhododendron bushes.

'Like what?' I questioned.

'Naked,' she answered abruptly as if I had failed to grasp the urgency of our predicament.

Naked, I thought. Well, it had never bothered us before, but now of course it was different and I found myself agreeing with her. Somehow, we needed to cover ourselves and hide from what we had done. I now recognise this as shame and guilt, something I had never experienced, and never wish anyone to ever experience.

We both hid behind the beautiful blossoming flowers. It was a great cover as we could see easily in all directions, but would be hidden from all who searched.

It was only a few minutes later we saw a shadow move in the distance.

'Adam,' a voice shouted.

Eve and I cowered behind the bush, dropping down lower and lower, but still keeping our Lord and friend in our sight. My chest was pounding so loudly I was sure that he would hear it even from the far-off distance. I could tell that Eve was feeling much the same. The twinkle had gone from her eyes, and there was a blank look on her face, which made me totally confused.

Eve moved closer and squatted beside me grabbing me by my arms as if trying to use me as shelter. Her skin was glistening with water droplets and felt damp; but I observed I was also the same. What could this possibly be? The feeling that I have come to recognise as guilt was so overwhelming, so consuming I felt as though my head and heart were about to explode. All these emotions were all completely new:

guilt, shame, regret, which of course were leading to the introduction of sin in our lives.

‘Adam! Where are you?’ the voice repeated.

I looked at Eve and she looked at me – for a split second we were locked in a somewhat panic.

‘We cannot hide in here for ever,’ I whispered into her ear.

She looked back at me blankly, and trembling she put her left hand on my shoulder and put a finger from her right hand in front of her lips to indicate to me to be quiet. Again, the same sense of emptiness came upon me. After all, the Lord was our friend and we were hiding from him. He had always shown us love and we were repaying him by hiding from him, knowing that we were in the wrong. He was our long-trusted friend, how could I ignore him now. I thought no matter what, even if we managed to ignore him today, what about tomorrow, the next day or even the next? Before I knew it, I stood up and peered over the rhododendron bush.

‘We are here, Lord, hiding.’ I said.

‘Hiding?’ he questioned.

‘Why are you hiding?’ he continued.

‘Because we didn’t want you to see our nakedness,’ I responded.

'Who told you, you were naked?' he questioned.

'Have you eaten from the tree from which I had told you not to eat?'

The Lord rebuked them both and then made garments to cover their nakedness.

It was clear the relationship between us had changed, and as I confessed to our mistakes, I could tell he was already aware fully of our actions.

As I now have the opportunity to look back, I can say that Eve and I had no excuse. We both let the aspect of our ego lead our way of thinking. We were easily led by the tempter and our pride was more about ourselves, more important at that stage than any relationship. We fell for the biggest con: "We could be like God."

I have to say at first I pointed the finger at Eve, as she had invited me to taste the fruit. I had a choice. I could have said no, but it was my own decision in the end and because of my own weakness I followed her suggestion. There was no doubt in the end it was my own choice.

I think for many people today it is easy to blame others for our mistakes, but in the final analysis, the choice is ours. As children we may be easily persuaded or directed in all we do, and as a child we are not always responsible for our decisions as we are as full-grown adults.

The clouds of doubt and darkness have hung over all mankind from this day. The joy and the freedom we both had are now replaced with the mist of doubt and sorrow.

I know as we sat in the presence of the Lord, his heart was broken and saddened by what we had done and that he fully understood the consequences of our actions, which would forever be a darkened spot on what was a special loving relationship. We sat for quite a while talking to the Lord and he shared his views openly, explaining how our actions had changed everything not just in his relationship with us but with all mankind. He loved us dearly, but our selfish actions had awakened sin within us. Sin had entered and now our special relationship was tainted.

New emotions crept over us as we opened ourselves to the knowledge of good and evil, and it was the evil element which had given birth within us. I suppose this is what is meant by ego - edging God out as we replace the goodness of all God had given for the emptiness of pain, sorrow, fear, anxiety and mistrust. Eventually this would lead to lies, hate, death and war, a far cry from the paradise we knew yesterday.

As in all cases we end up with the “if” statements. If only I didn’t do, If only I hadn’t said, if only I hadn’t trusted; the list goes on and on.

Life has changed drastically for Eve and me. We opened up the case of what God calls 'free will' – instead of keeping the love and trust in God we chose differently because we thought we knew better.

It is funny but in all that has happened I knew the Lord would love us no matter what, but we were responsible for our own actions and our own lives; we knew the Lord would always be there for us, but never in the same way.

The Lord explained the punishment for our action. We were to be banished from Eden, our lovely home, from the paradise we knew. Toil and sweat were to be our burden now. The enjoyment and pleasure had been replaced by sweat and pain. This demonstrates the curse of following yourself and not God, that often in life you will find you are crushed, taken away from the good and the lush and thrown in the midst of a self-interested curse.

Then there was the expulsion from paradise, the banishment from Eden and our place of freedom and care, to be lost in a world that didn't care. Our place of love was now thrown into the unknown.

The Lord tearfully had explained the consequences of our actions it was true, but, in short it was ourselves who were only to blame; we invoked the sins and the curse, which we truly accepted in a blind sore of lust. The whole of humanity and creation too was blemished forever and there was nothing we could do. There was no return, no easy path for us to follow.

The Lord explained to us that we had broken the chain of innocence and trust, bringing in with it greed, jealousy and pride.

The trust and love of our friend with a childlike heart who loved us and shared with us fun, excitement and above all his safety, his love should have been sufficient for us, but our selfish desires to be just like him brought us only pain and sorrow.

We had in turn taken our relationship from trust and love in friendship, which met our every need, to choosing to walk the path alone without him, in just a silly whim. From a fruitful friendship to an empty chasm. The Lord created us as the icing on the cake of his creation, but allowed us to be free. In trust and love we flourished, to throwing it away on what he called our own free will.

I had tried to argue the case that he gave us the option of choice. He did but without choice, there would be no freedom and no trust - only a dictatorship. We would not be free, but senseless beings without the ability to make our own decisions or mistakes. You could argue, I thought, that we didn't know better; but then that is the point: we have to learn to trust and put our faith in our friend. In the end we didn't trust or put our trust in him, we simply wanted to be the same or better than he was.

The Lord gave us a choice and we took our chance to try and gain everything, but in the end our action led to our downfall.

Banishment from paradise, sent from the Garden of Eden was much harder than we could have ever imagined.

We had been provided for. But now we were clothed and set to live and provide for ourselves without the real comforts of his protection. Yes, we had to work in Eden, but never like we have to now. Don't get me wrong, our banishment from Eden wasn't into a barren landscape; but it very much seemed like it.

After our departure and farewell we set off with heavy hearts, both of us not saying very much, neither of us trying to blame one another, but all the time knowing it was our decision, our free will. We defied the Lord and now we began to understand the void we had shaped in our lives. We began to understand the human nature of self- greed and self-determination to be equals; but equal we could never be.

We wandered off and eventually came to a flat portion of land next to the river. Several times we had stopped and looked back knowing life was about to change completely.

We decided to make our home in a small rock crag, a very small cave not far from the trees and the river. It became our shelter. We tried bitterly to convince each other it was nice and adequate for our needs. This was the start of a very steep learning curve in how to survive. Now we had to find our own food, learn to cook and start to grow food.

We had been out of Eden for only a couple of days when the hunger pains really struck. Several times we had eaten berries or leaves that made us unwell; I wish I had taken more care in observing what we had eaten in Eden. The bounty we had before became the focal point in our daily task of trying to survive, never had I imagined how different it would be.

I had found a little rock base at the side of the river where I could sit and spend time alone, contemplating, praying, reflecting. This became my favourite spot where I planned for a better future.

"Adam." A voice in the distance. I looked round in anticipation for a moment thinking it was the Lord, but soon realised it was Eve calling.

"Are you going to sit there all day? Or are you going to find food to eat?" she questioned.

To think we wanted to be like the Lord, but now we are slaves to our survival.

We had everything, it was all ours, but now we have nothing but our independence and freedom, but at what cost.

This is our free will and our curse, which eventually led to what we now call sin.

The hardest part of temptation is learning that we can say no; but ego, we learn, makes things look so promising, so tempting it attracts our greed and our rational thought if we allow it.

But by saying yes to it leads only to sadness, emptiness and guilt, something I didn't think I had chosen. However, I am afraid to say it comes as a package, a package our choice laid before us always.

I encourage you today in my garden of sorrow – to seek the garden of peace and learn to trust in the Lord knowing that if you choose to walk your own way, it will lead only to sorrow.

A Lazy Day in the Garden.

Okay, I am sitting here in the garden for a lazy day on my own; coffee at hand and a couple of biscuits, a custard cream and a ginger nut; all set to do my own thing. The sun is shining, and all is well in the world, well in my garden anyway.

I have often thought the phraseology we use in our everyday life is a bit peculiar, but we all use it. Take my statement, the sun is shining; well obviously because that is what the sun does. It is nothing but an average-sized yellow star. It is one of the most common type of star in the universe. It is truly a cosmic furnace: hydrogen atoms under unimaginable pressures are being fused into helium atoms, releasing a tremendous amount of energy, which comes to us as a large glow in the sky with an intense heat for our solar system. Because of its lovely warmth, I bask in the comfortable 20° C but on the surface of the sun it is a staggering 6,000° C, which would mean I would need more than Factor 15 sun oil. Often, we say things like, 'I hope the sun shines today,' or 'Brill, the sun is coming out!' when in truth the sun always is because, if it wasn't there, we would not be here. In a real sense, the reason we do not see so much of the sun in the northern hemisphere is our orbit position in space and our angle on the planet. The weather has a lot to do with it too; the good old clouds. There are places on our planet where the sun shines every day, but then, they don't have the lush green environment I have in my garden today.

Well, today the sun is out. It is a lovely warm day and I am going to enjoy it.

I take a sip of my coffee and dip my ginger nut biscuit into it -- not too much, as I don't want to have half of it dislodged in the bottom of my cup. I take it out and suck the wet coffee-flavoured biscuit. A sense of bliss runs through my veins. The sheer enjoyment tantalizes my taste buds.

A little finch chirps as it hops past my feet. It is a scruffy little bird, but quite friendly. It is often running around when we are in the garden. It has a somewhat crooked tail. It has a nice brown coat, with white markings down its side, showing that it is truly from the finch family. It has a high-pitched squeak or whistle for such a small bird and it is amusing to observe as it moves around my feet. It is funny the way its body moves as it jerks along the ground, chirping all the time.

I hear the cows mooing in the field down from the house. Something must have upset them as they don't always give such a roar -- well only when the calves are taken away from their mothers. I am glad we live far enough from the cow shed when that happens as the cows bellow 24 hours a day for days following the separation; it's bad enough just hearing the sounds in the distance, never mind staying in the cottage next to the sheds.

The telephone rings in the house, but I am determined to ignore it; nothing will pull me away from my lazy day and my peaceful time. Eventually the telephone stops ringing and the silence returns. I relax now, happy the intrusion has gone. I have always felt the telephone is one of these items which has no manners. It always seems to ring at the most awkward or quiet time. Mind you, it would be funny if it did occasionally say, ‘Would you mind awfully if I interrupt you?’

No matter what, it is amazing how the nagging brain challenges you to check to see who called! What if it was something important? But I stay strong to my task and remain where I am. I lean forward and take another sip of coffee.

The woodpecker has decided to put in an appearance, helping himself to the nuts from the feeder, which hangs from the washing line. Its headbanging is funny to watch as he tries to get to the nuts inside the wire cage. A pigeon walks below, hoping to catch all the bits that fall, letting the woodpecker do all the demanding work. However, as I lean forward to place my coffee down, he is off, as any sudden movement triggers danger and he heads into the heights of the tree for safety. Several small birds return, mostly sparrows and take the place of the woodpecker. I sit back in my chair and enjoy the scene. They are having what would be their version of afternoon coffee.

There are several fluffy clouds. These are the big 'fluffy' clouds that look a bit like cotton balls. I think they are called cumulus clouds. They tend to indicate that the atmosphere is unstable at the altitude where they are found; so hopefully they will pass over quickly and allow me to enjoy my time in the garden. All is well as there seems to be plenty of blue sky. We refer to the sky as blue, but in real terms it is just an illusion. The sky looks blue because when the sun is overhead, the atmosphere scatters more blue light than any other colour, so the colour that reaches our eyes is blue!

A tractor passes by, disturbing my thought pattern. It goes down the dirt track at the side of the cottage and the garden. It throws up dust all over the place. The weather has been dry for a few weeks, so the constant dust from passing vehicles usually covers the windows of the cottage, not to mention the car. The driver of the tractor waves. I wave back but I am unable to see him clearly owing to the light of the sun which is directly behind him.

The garden is looking lovely as it is in full colour with all the flowers bursting forth in all their glory, not to mention all the green from the vegetable garden, lovingly looked after by my wife. But today, well at least at this moment, I am the sole occupant of the garden, left in charge of its very existence, so what better way to observe it all than to sit lazily on my chair and enjoy.

I close my eyes to rest my weary mind, but it doesn't last long as I am disturbed by the relentless cooing of the ever-present pigeons. Their rhetoric sounds to me like the sound of an owl being strangled whilst trying to hoot, and it only starts off a little chain reaction as others join in too, in the distance.

My little friend, the robin, turns up for a quick look at me, or maybe he is more interested in my uneaten custard cream! I stretch forward, claim my custard cream and take a bite. Then take a mouthful of coffee and finish the biscuit for its safe-keeping. It is safely consigned now to my bodily functions and the taste swirls round my mouth.

The robin leaps about in his quizzical manner. I try to whistle to him, but it comes out like a poor gasp of air and no real pitch sound to it. He stops, tilts his head, looks at me and then carries on in his distinct way.

A couple of goldfinch fight each other for the delights of the Niger seed, which means neither of them has any peace to eat. They spend most of their time chasing each other. At last one remains, but he then spends most of his time watching and waiting for the slightest movement, before flying off again. These little birds are charming and fun to watch; their vibrant colours cause them to stand out among most other birds. But they are very timid, and it doesn't take much for them to be startled.

The robin sits on the edge of my upturned box, my deluxe garden coffee table. He looks intently at me then flies off into the trees at the far end of the garden.

I stretch out my legs and, after another sip of my coffee, rest my eyes again from the bright sunlight. The passing sound of the post van disturbs me; I open my eyes a little, see the red van and return to the comfort of my snooze. The van driver has gone next door, so it will be a few minutes until he arrives at our door should we have any post. Eyes closed again, I feel the warmth of the sun and relax. The next thing I know, the garden gate opens:

Hi-ya,' the postman shouts as he enters the garden.

He waves to me and throws the couple of letters on the mat inside the open front door.

'Lovely day again,' he remarks.

I manage to get myself together to respond.

'Yes, it is,' I call, smiling and waving back at him. He goes out the gate and closes it.

'Enjoy your peace and quiet,' he comments as he returns to his van.

‘Thanks,’ I respond, thinking to myself, well it was peaceful and quiet before you arrived. His van speeds off to deliver next door and I return to my relaxed position.

I finish the remnants of my coffee and another tractor speeds down the lane. The driver waves and I wave back. Everyone around where we live is very friendly; everyone waves, even if you don’t know who they are.

Most of the birds in the garden have scurried to the trees for safety as the tractor passes. The dust is tossed through the air like a whirlwind or sand being blown over the desert. I sit quite glad that my position is far enough away from its effects so that I am not covered in it.

I return to my seat, sitting back and relaxing once again, waiting not just for the dust but also for my awakened mind to settle. I try and drift off in my thoughts, enjoying the peace and quiet.

As I sit with my eyes closed, feeling the sunshine encase me in its warmth, I hear birds chirping away, always a pleasant sound, very calming and for some strange reason soothing.

The pigeons are quiet for a change. I can hear the faint noise of an aircraft overhead. We often get planes passing. The jets are so high we just see the little dot of the plane and the jet stream. Occasionally military jets fly low between the hills. Their sound is painful on the ears, and often they are miles away before we hear them. The smaller planes are usually one-engine training aircraft. But even these small aeroplanes make quite a noise. They often switch off the engine and glide for a while and then restart the engine, preferably before they meet the ground. I suppose it is much safer to fly over farm land than over highly populated areas for training.

I hear a hawk screech. I look up in the sky and there sure enough is a hawk. It is circling high in the sky, taking in the air currents as it scans the ground for prey. They look magnificent as they glide through the air in full wing span. Their special brown markings stand out for all to see. I watch as it circles. Then like a bullet it dives at full speed to the ground. It must have spotted prey.

I read once that hawks have four types of colour receptors in the eye. These give them the ability to perceive not only the visible range but also the ultraviolet part of the spectrum. A hawk's diet is predictable and includes a variety of smaller animals like snakes, lizards, fish, mice, rabbits, squirrels, birds, and any other type of small game that is found on the ground. However, as the hawk speeds to the ground, I lose sight of it owing to the contours of the ground. It is amazing that they can spot prey from so high in the sky.

I look around the garden, my patience with this relaxing lark seems to be growing thin and I begin to think of things I could get up and do. I lean forward and rise from my chair. Well I suppose I could start with checking the mail and see who called.

As I march towards the house, I think to myself, I could always have another cup of coffee and another five minutes. Sounds like a plan, I think.

Ten minutes later I find myself back in the chair with my coffee in hand. The phone call was a number I didn't recognise so it was probably a call centre. The mail, both letters were junk mail, so I filed them in the recycle bin.

It takes me a while to settle again, but settle I do. It could be the caffeine! But hey, I enjoy it, so I relax and enjoy the sun and its warm rays. The peaceful surroundings help me to relax once again, as I slowly drop into my comfort mode.

I spot the red squirrel on the squirrel box. He is helping himself to the nuts inside. He perches himself on top of the box holding the nut in his claws as he eats it. His bright red rusty coloured tail arches over his back to his head before he disappears back into the box for more nuts. Several birds are on the bird feeder which hangs from the branch of the tree just a few feet from the squirrel. Both feeding groups are happy and content at their filling stations. It's a lovely sight just to sit and watch. The speed and agility of the squirrel are fantastic.

I hear children playing in the distance. It's the children next door, enjoying fun in the warm weather as they chase after each other. It takes me back to my parenthood days when my children were young. Seems like a century ago now; how time flies. The years just seem to drift by without a thought of how life has changed. One minute you can be working every hour possible to make ends meet; and the next you are sitting down to take a breath and find yourself thinking back to bygone years; the children have grown up and have children of their own.

The laugher turns to crying as one of the boys seems to be unhappy with his lot.

My mind returns to the squirrel as it comes back out from recovering another nut and he sits proudly on the top eating away quite happily. Then he is off; something must have startled him! I wonder was it the child crying? But no, a land rover appears. It is the farmer driving down the lane. His dog sits on the front seat leaning out the window and taking in the rush of air. The driver waves and gives a big hearty smile. I return the gesture and wave back.

Then a distant bang. It was definitely a gun shot. It must be the gamekeeper out shooting pigeons, or it could be at the dreaded crows? Over the past week there have been hundreds of crows about. They must be feasting on the recently cut pea field.

A couple of butterflies flutter past me, floating by without a care in the world. I also observe a couple of cabbage white butterflies down at the bottom of the garden. They had better stay away from the cabbage and broccoli.

I sit back with my coffee cup, take another few sips and then return it to my coffee table. My mind starts to wonder again. The reason I know the sun has moved round in the sky is that I am now in the shade. I change my seating to be back in the sunlight.

It is amazing how different things are as you look at them from various angles. The same thing can be said about life. If only people would in times of trouble and problems take time to look at the situation in another way, and, with a different perspective, be able to do something about it rather than sticking to a negative complaining mode. Stuff happens in life. It isn't easy at times, but we must just fix it, or accept it and move forward.

Suddenly, I hear a car horn. It is the gamekeeper coming up the lane in his little white van. He gives a big smile and a hearty wave as he always does. I wave back smiling, acknowledging him as we always do. He looks happy, mind you he always does, but I think he has managed to get a few hits with his shot gun. I laugh as I notice a pheasant in next door's garden and wonder if I should tell it to hide although it is safe for the time being. Pheasant shooting season is not for another six months or so.

Soon I drift back, closing my eyes and enjoying the warmth of the sun once again. The sunshine on my face is most welcome. The light twinkles in my eyes with my eyelids closed and I feel myself drift deeper into a sleep, and the doze mode.

Warmth and peace come over me and for a few seconds I drift into a heavenly plane, happily into my warm and safe place.

After a few moments I awaken, looking at the birds all around the garden, also enjoying the day. Mr Bullfinch has also made an appearance. The male bullfinch is unmistakable with his bright pinkish-red breast and cheeks, grey back, black cap and tail, and bright white rump. He is quite elegant as he moves around the ground underneath the nut feeder picking up all the scraps on the grass.

I sit straight up, check to see if I have any coffee left, but no, it is finished.

The telephone rings again.

I rise and set off for the house to answer the call.

It has been a lovely day today, but time passes and duty calls.

I look to the sky and say to myself, ‘Don’t go away, Mr. Sunshine. I plan to be back tomorrow.’

Garden of Peace and Sorrows.

Gethsemane

There standing before me is the great Mount of Olives, which we have come to know so well.

This narrow range of peaks which overlook the ancient city of Jerusalem; it stretches out through the Kidron Valley -- Kid'ron in Hebrew means dusky, gloomy.

Looking down on this wondrous city towards the ancient Golden Gate (Eastern Gate), we see the Pool of Siloam. In ancient times this valley would have been heavily wooded, but today it is much more open, giving a glorious view into the Garden of Gethsemane, which is east of Jerusalem at the foot of the Mount of Olives.

Most of the trees were cut down during the reign of the Roman leader, Titus.

The garden of Gethsemane measures 50 square metres and dates back to the seventh century BCE. At that time, it would have been more open; part of the main garden area was later walled by Franciscan monks in 1848.

The term Gethsemane means olive grove or olive press mill and is named from the trees which are located on the Mount of Olives.

It is ironic but true that we see not only olives being crushed in this place but also at a later time, our Lord's spirit being crushed as he prepared himself for what we call the Passion, the bending of his will (free will) to the will of the Father, which eventually led to his death on the cross.

Up to this time the Garden of Gethsemane was seen as a retreat for Jesus and his disciples on their visits to Jerusalem. We read in Luke's Gospel the words, "Jesus went as usual to the Mount of Olives, and his disciples followed him."(Luke 22:39) This would have been considered a place of peace, a place of prayer and reflection after the business and bustle of Jerusalem; but in the end for Jesus, it became a place of sorrow and anguish.

Jesus often went to places of solitude for prayer and reflection, and Gethsemane was one of these places. The trip to the garden was a time of refreshment not only for Jesus but for his disciples too. This was a place where they were able to rest and enjoy the quiet and serenity. One of the common rituals we see of Jesus is Jesus kneeling to pray (Luke 22:41), something we see within the church even today.

There are several mentions of Gethsemane in the New Testament, some of which we will look at later.

But first let us consider portions of the teaching known as The Olivet Discourse, which took place here in Gethsemane on the Tuesday before Jesus's death on Friday.

The Olivet Discourse is the last major section of teaching by Jesus, as recorded in Matthew, Mark, and Luke (Matthew 24:3-25:46; Mark 13:3-37; Luke 21:5-36). It deals with the signs of Christ's return and events associated with it. Matthew has the longest version and begins with the disciples asking Jesus when the Temple will be destroyed, when Christ will return, and what will be the end of the age (Matthew 24:3). The is preceded by Jesus exposing the hypocrisy and false teachings of the Pharisees (Matthew 23:1-39; Mark 12:13-40; Luke 20:1-47). In Matthew it is followed by the parable of the 10 virgins (Matthew 25:1-13), the parable of the talents (Matthew 25:14-30), and the judgment that will come with Christ's return (Matthew 25:31-46).

As we read the disclosures, we see that Jesus had taught mostly in Parables, a common form of teaching at that time. This challenged the listener to determine the true meaning and message that was being put forward. It invited the hearers always to seek the truth, and know the truth for themselves, rather than just be given the information which then could be easily forgotten or disregarded. Jesus through his teaching wants us to find the hidden truth in all we do; and we can only do that if we open our hearts and minds to seeking the truths for ourselves, and then finding a means of illustrating profound, divine truths to help in our daily devotions and our walks with the Lord. Parables are easily remembered, the characters are bold, and the symbolism is rich in meaning. Parables were a common form of teaching in Judaism. Before a certain point in his ministry, Jesus had employed many graphic analogies, using everyday items that would be familiar to everyone (salt, bread, sheep,) and their meaning was fairly clear in the context of his teaching.

We read about the warning to the Pharisees, the falseness of their actions, which would lead to the destruction of all they believed in, especially the Temple itself. The disclosures contain references to future events. They are also known as the Little Apocalypse because they include the use of apocalyptic language and Jesus's warning to his followers that they will suffer tribulation and persecution before the ultimate triumph of the Kingdom of God.

On Friday (John 18:2) Jesus walks from the upper room to the garden. This would have taken him through the Golden Gate (Eastern Gate) and across the brook which was called Cedron, or black brook, because it was well known to be tainted by the dirt of the city.

The Passion

We see Jesus and the eleven disciples departing the upper room after the Passover celebrations. The mood would have been somewhat confusing for the disciples. After all, the Passover was a celebration of faith and deliverance of the nation of Israel, and therefore a joyous time for their identity and existence. They were God's chosen people and the celebrations showed what it all entailed, for them to go from slavery to free people in their God.

The mood would have been sombre. There was the washing of the feet, the celebration meal, to the declarations that his life, Jesus' life, was about to be taken from them by a traitor. Not only that but Jesus had told Peter that a time would come when he would deny even knowing him. This would have seemed obscure even for Peter at this time. There was also a demonstration of what we now call the Lord's supper, with Jesus naming the bread to be his body and wine to be his blood. What did this mean for the disciples? What were they to make of what he was saying, what was the meaning behind his teaching?

They made their way out of the city across the brook into the Kidron Valley, into the olive grove and the garden.

The mood must have seemed heavy. We are told the disciples could hardly keep their eyes open, never mind stay alert. Everything over the previous few days had been so hectic. After all, this was Jerusalem. The city was packed to bursting point because of the Passover celebrations. This was a real headache for all the city authorities, especially the Romans, who knew a small spark could start a riot.

Did the disciples really understand the severity of the events as they entered the garden. By their actions one would assume not. Were their minds only focussed on the need to sleep? Were they confused about everything? Were they in considerable turmoil at everything that had taken place and what they had been told?

As Jesus and the disciples entered the garden, he gestured for most of them to settle in one place. He then took Peter, James and John further into the garden and instructed them to sit and pray, but their minds were so heavy and overwhelmed that they fell asleep.

Jesus had moved forwarded into a clearing and fell down on his knees in anguish and prayed. The disciples must have observed the torment and the heartache Jesus was experiencing. Did they not see his anguish? My thoughts would be that they were so lost in their own tiredness that they missed the clues of the pain and agony of Jesus.

The isolation Jesus must have felt would have been overwhelming as he fell to his knees, feeling that the weight of the whole world's sins was upon his shoulders. The aspect of fear and death would have been harrowing as he knelt to pray.

"Father take this cup from me!"

How often have we prayed in this way for ourselves for some personal course rather than a life-saving plea?

Jesus knew the cup of suffering being offered to him was the cup of his own suffering and death. Yes, earlier Jesus had invited the disciples to drink from the cup, representing his blood laid out for them. But now, it was his own true blood which Jesus was about to give, the cup of his suffering, and like us, he would have preferred to have an easier way, but he continued his prayer,

"Not my will, but your will."

How difficult it is to subordinate your will to someone else's will, especially when you know what you are taking on, as you surrender your own self to it. This is what Jesus had just agreed to do - surrender his will to do the will of the Father, even though he knew it would lead to a painful death. So, by consenting to bend his will, he was in fact saying:

"Father I surrender to you and allow you to do as you want, not because I want to; but because I must, no matter what it will cost."

The anguish, pain, fears, suffering would have been entirely agonising. In fact, we are told that the anguish and pain he was suffering at this time made his sweat run with blood (Luke 22:44). I can scarcely imagine the torment and fear he was feeling with the terror that would be building up within him. I know all too much about the anguish, upset, the feeling of nausea, the inner feeling of terror within; but this is nothing in comparison with the real anguish of what Jesus was undergoing.

Blood like sweatlets ran down his face as his blood pressure rose to burst blood vessels. This condition, known as hematidrosis, also called blood sweat, is very rare, where a human sweats blood. The term is from Ancient Greek meaning blood and sweat. According to the National Health Service website, the condition is rare. Blood usually oozes from the forehead, nails, umbilicus, and other skin surfaces. In addition, oozing from mucocutaneous surfaces causing nosebleeds, blood-stained tears, and vicarious menstruation is common. The episodes may be preceded by intense headache and abdominal pain and are usually self-limiting. In some conditions, the secreted fluid is partly diluted and appears to be blood-tinged, while others may have darker bright red secretions resembling blood. While the extent of blood loss generally is minimal, hematidrosis also results in the skin becoming extremely tender and fragile.

Jesus knew there was another way, his own way, or as we would say, my way. His free will meant he had the option of getting up and walking away; however, Jesus knew what was at stake here. The Father had sent him to do his will in order to bring all humanity back to himself, and so he had no other thought than doing what his Father had sent him to do.

Jesus was to offer himself as a living sacrifice. He knew there was more at stake than just his life. He knew that, no matter what, he was to offer himself for the sins of all mankind. To give his life for all. He states this in Matthew 20:28;

“Just as the Son of Man did not come to be served, but to serve, and to give his life as a ransom for many.”

Again, in Mark 10:45;

“For even the Son of Man did not come to be served, but to serve, and to give his life as a ransom for many."

And again, in John;

“Greater love has no one than this: to lay down one's life for one's friends.”

Thy Will Be Done

Jesus wept and anguished over his prayer, “... not my will, but thy will be done.”

He taught this to his disciples in the prayer that we call the Lord's prayer, '... your kingdom come, your will be done on earth as it is in heaven." (Mathew 6:9). Jesus knew the importance of this statement and here he puts it into action.

He rose from his pain and suffering and went back to his disciples, Peter, James and John. However, when he arrived beside them, he found they had fallen asleep. How heartbroken he must have been - his closest friends and colleagues had fallen asleep at this very testing time.

"Why are you sleeping?" he asked them. "Get up and pray you do not fall into temptation." (Luke 22:46 and Matthew 26:40f).

In Matthew we are told Jesus went back to pray and again he returned to find the disciples asleep. How often do we fail in our walk because we do not understand the true significance of what is taken place?

I often wonder if the words of Mordecai to Queen Esther were in focus at this time. Mordecai said to Esther that maybe she had 'come to royal position for such a time as this?' This was Jesus time. Then it was Esther time, and now Jesus was faced with the task of bringing redemption, not just to the Jews, but to the whole of mankind. This was his time; this was his greatest test, and his love for the Father would not be broken even though he knew he himself would be broken, crushed and crucified for all mankind.

"Not my will, but your will," he repeated.

Consider the disciples -- we may question their friendship, their loyalty, but it is all too easy to sit as judge and jury. After all, we are reminded in Matthew 7 that Jesus taught, "Do not judge, or you too will be judged. For in the same way you judge others, you will be judged." It is not for us to criticise others when in fact we would have more than likely done the same thing. It is always easier to say you would not! But when it comes to the test, how often do we stagger and fall.

Judgment on others is not our mission; judgment is for the Father. We seek to bring humanity to the foot of the cross and repentance before God, just as Jesus was doing in this situation. The very cross where Jesus was to be crucified is now the place where the forgiveness of sins had experienced victory because Jesus was loyal to his Father and to his wishes.

Having returned to prayer, Jesus again accepted the will of the Father over his own free will. The garden of peace, Gethsemane, was now truly a garden of sorrows, but also a garden of victory. This was a very isolated place as there were no friends to help; this was truly a walk of faith and a giving of sacrificial love.

The Hour Comes

As he arose and made his way back to his disciples, Jesus would have seen lights and torches approaching in the distance. The lighted torches shone out to his pending trial and fears. He could have run, he could have disappeared, vanished and escaped it all; but the words 'not my will, but yours!' was the underlying commitment to stand firm and trust in the Father.

He woke the disciples.

"Are you still sleeping, and resting? Enough! The hour has come. Look, the Son of Man is betrayed into the hands of sinners. Rise! Let us go! Here comes my betrayer." (Mark 14: 41 – 42).

There he stood looking at the approaching mob, seeking to bring about his impending judgment.

The temple guards, dressed in their full military uniform, carried torches in one hand and clubs or swords in the other. They anticipated a riot and Jesus met them in peace.

Their faces were solemn as they marched in unison with the intent of completing their task no matter the cost. Beside them was a small mob, set on violence, ready for a fight, laden with their own clubs and mazes. Unlike the guards who were doing their job, they were intent on a fight, so the slightest spark would enforce their anger. It didn't matter toward whom, or what it was about, they just wanted to follow the cause, what we call today a small vigilantly group ready to fight for any cause.

Jesus' focus changed as his gaze took in the other slight figure who was there, Judas. This was a figure he knew, a man he knew well, a man he loved, a man he had chosen to be one of his inner twelve, a man he knew from this day on would always have his name known as a traitor, a name of betrayal.

Without doubt Jesus would have recalled his thoughts, knowing the outcome, not just for what would happen to him, but also to his betrayer, Judas Iscariot.

"But woe to that man who betrays the Son of Man! It would be better for him if he had not been born." (Mark 14: 21).

If we reflect on the mixed emotions of it all, we can see the aspect of the fear and trembling; to love and yet be broken-hearted by his friend and disciple. The emotional conflicts with the blood-sweating skin produce tears of sadness and betrayal.

The disciples had just risen to their feet as the mob arrived. For a split second or two, their focus would have been on the mob and then on Jesus; their hearts were full now of fear and wonder, what was about to happen?

The angry mob came to a stop at a distance. Jesus and the disciples watched the motley crew before them, the darkness making it difficult to weigh up the coming confrontation. For an instant there was silence as both sides looked at each other. The mob was ready, full of adrenaline waiting for the trigger for action.

The disciples half asleep looking intently at the crowds and at Jesus.

Jesus' focus was fixed totally on Judas.

Judas, knowing looked directly at Jesus sheepishly; he was very uneasy. But he had arranged this confrontation and now he had to see it through.

Judas turned to the soldier in charge. He then clasped his hands in front of him. He moved forward, lifted his right hand and pushed the hair from his sweating brow. He felt anxious as he stepped forward towards Jesus.

Jesus made a slight step forward only to move into the light. The disciples gazed at Jesus, then Judas and the crowd. It was clear to them that something drastic was about to happen.

Judas moved forward,

"Going at once to Jesus, Judas said, "Rabbi!" and kissed him. The men seized Jesus and arrested him. Then one of those standing near drew his sword and struck the servant of the high priest, cutting off his ear. "Am I leading a rebellion," said Jesus, "that you have come out with swords and clubs to capture me? Every day I was with you, teaching in the Temple courts, and you did not arrest me. But the Scriptures must be fulfilled." Then everyone deserted him and fled."

It was clear the kiss was the signal for the soldiers to know which man to arrest.

The Temple guards attempted to control the crowds. During the confusion, the disciples ran off leaving Jesus, bound and alone with the guards and the mob.

The soldiers pushed Jesus forward to lead him away after they had tied him up. Their job was done and now they just had to return him to Jerusalem and the high priest.

Judas stood there frozen as everything had gone far beyond what he had expected. He was no longer needed; the guards ignored him and moved off. Judas saw his friend and master now a sad figure, mocked by the guards and the mob. He had not expected this, his master an object of jokes, mockery and anger from the crowds looking for blood. It had not gone the way he had intended. He gave a deep sigh, looked at the crowds and started to follow.

Then in a sudden fateful moment, Jesus turned and looked directly at Judas. This caught Judas by surprise as it seemed the Lord was looking directly at his soul, His eyes piercing his heart, eyes of sorrow and pain but also eyes of love and without blame – only sorrow and perhaps pity. Judas' heart sank even deeper amid his confusion and frustration at what he had brought about. It was then that the whole situation hit him. The pain of it all he never thought possible. Tears flowed down his master's face, and now tears flowed down his face. What had he done?

"Come on, move along." The guards shouted and pushed Jesus to force him to move forward. They wanted him off of their hands, their job done now, time to get back to the barracks. Jesus nearly fell at the force that had been inflicted. Unable to use his hands to help steady himself, he fell to the ground and the guards quickly pushed and shoved him back to his feet.

"Come on, come on. We haven't got all night." They shouted.

Jesus turned and staggered forward, stepping out of the garden which had been one of peace, which will now always be remembered as the garden of sorrows.

What had been a place of friendship, peace and prayer now was to be known as a garden of sorrow, pain anguish and betrayal.

However, the Garden of Gethsemane was also to be known as the place of victory, the place where Jesus gave his own will over to the Father's, and became the Saviour of the whole world.

The Garden of Gethsemane, a place of Peace to Sorrows to a place of true Passion.

The Garden of Peace and Sorrows
The Garden of Choice

I base the stories in this book on and around gardens. Gardens are places which clearly play a big part in our daily lives.

Gardens can be places of beauty and wonder. But also, they can be overgrown, unsightly and barren. They can be places of peace and relaxation, but also places of sweat and toil.

The contrast is always clear to see between a well-kept garden and one which is neglected. We could say gardens are a reflection of ourselves, how we live our lives.

However, this can only be an outward indication of how we truly are in everything we do. Some people like their gardens filled with beautiful flowers, some with an abundance of vegetables and fruit. Others see little need for any care, happily letting the garden grow wild while some are content to concrete over the garden to ensure a maintenance-free zone. Can these types of garden be reflected in our own life styles?

We can give the appearance of being well-mannered and orderly but, deep within ourselves, we know this can be far from the truth. It is often the case that people suffering from a serious illness, depression or sadness can still give the impression that everything is well when this is far from the case.

In concluding this book, I want to look at three gardens in particular, The Garden of Eden (the garden of failure and sin), The Garden of Gethsemane (the garden of passion, sorrows and victory) and finally The Garden of Choice.

The similarities and differences between Eden and Gethsemane cannot be overstated. In the first instance, in Eden, we see Adam (the first Adam) living in a beautiful garden of peace, love and friendship with the Lord. Then there is temptation, followed by the anguish of Adam (as well as Eve) as he failed the test in his walk with the Lord, choosing to go his own way and so being banished from the garden for his sin and rebellion as punishment from the Lord.

In contrast, we see Jesus (the bible refers to Jesus being the second Adam .The Apostle Paul tells us in his first letter to the church in Corinth, "The first man Adam became a living being; the last Adam, a life-giving spirit. The spiritual did not come first, but the natural, and after that the spiritual." Therefore Jesus would be the second Adam in scripture), also placed within a garden of beauty (Gethsemane), which at first was a place of peace and love. But in this case the eventual anguish is not of defiance but of obedience, not anguish of failure and rejection but of being willing to be faithful and putting his trust in the Father rather than self. And so, it becomes a victory over temptation and acceptance and in turn is fully rewarded by the Father.

The first Adam failed the Lord. The second Adam honoured the Father, but both had to face their own anguish and make their own decisions.

How often do we need to face these same decisions in our lives? We are confronted with the anguish of sin, temptation and our own will, which is being tested to the limit in our lives daily. Both gardens offered peace and love, but in all things, peace and love always come at a price. It is our free will to choose. We can opt either for our own free will, or the way of the Lord in truth and faith, resisting the world's folly and fake promises. Both paths bring us anguish which we have to go through; both have consequences. One path leaves us alone and the other gives us the love of the Father and the peace which helps us to walk our daily walk with him. One path leads to death and separation (self-ego), separation from God and expulsion from his care while the other causes us to bend, to follow his will (salvation), which places us still in this world, but with his care, love and protection in all we do. In the end, we have to make our own choices and face our own garden experiences. One path brings joy and love, the other emptiness and anguish.

I am not much of a gardener myself, although I do try. I leave most of the gardening to my wife who is much keener to look after the growing of the flowers, vegetables and fruit whereas I cut, trim the grass and help with the heavy lifting and occasional digging, as well as looking after our much-welcomed feathered friends and squirrels.

Gardens take a lot of looking after and maintenance. However, the joys of the work are plain for all to see and the taste of the fruit and vegetables always seems much more pleasant than shop varieties, making all the labour much more rewarding.

Our lives require much the same type of maintenance. Like the garden, if we don't watch and care for our lives, the weeds will always sprout and cut off the very life within the garden and within us.

Our two stories of gardens, Eden and Gethsemane, in this book pointed out the contrast between the two. Some choices are easy: to eat the fruit of temptation or not to. For the harder decisions, when you know what is the proper and true choice to make, it can be the most difficult thing to do. The easiest option is not always the best one.

We all have gardens of some type. Mostly I think people love them. There is nothing lovelier to look at than a well-kept garden.

Big stately gardens can be very formal and regimental. This can be great to view but not always be to our taste. Other gardens can be very well looked after, but are wild and carefree; again, it is all about taste. Then again there are the gardens which are overgrown, with no concept of what is where or how it should be. Some may like this, but it is the first two that require considerable sweat and toil, loving tender care while the garden which is never worked or cared for quickly grows over to become unsightly and covered in nettles and thorns.

As I write this at the end of March the garden is aglow with colour. The snowdrops have just died and the daffodils are in bloom for all to see. The heather is flowering and so is the primula.

It's the start of a new adventure of spring bursting into life after the hard, cold winter; the joys of spring bring forth the hope of a nice warm summer. Living in the country we are blessed with many visitors in the garden. As you could tell by the story of a lazy day in the garden (one of the stories also contained with The Garden book of stories). We have many feathered friends such as woodpeckers, pheasants, partridges, as well as squirrels, coming and going all the time.

We look out onto fields and hills, so we see crops starting to grow. The soil turns from its winter brownness to different shades of green.

At the end of March, we are always fascinated with the wild life. Today I saw six hares running in the field in front of the house, as their mating season gets underway and the odd boxing competition comes into play.,

It will not be long before the cows will make their reproach to their winter shut-in, when they were not able to enjoy the freedom of outside because of being inside, away from the cold and damp.

Life in the country and life in the garden are inseparably linked. Time rolls on whether we like it or not. No matter if you are a gardener or not, you cannot get away from the beauty of the seasons and the great wonder of it all.

Yes, creation is undoubtedly a wonder, which we are all privileged to share. We watch the transformation from winter to spring, spring to summer and summer to autumn, bringing an array of different colours no matter what the season, from the winter cold to the summer heat, from the blossoming flowers to the leaf-starved trees.

On reflection, the garden can be used as a metaphor for our lives and our moods. The cold dull days of the inner barren landscape, the struggling of life with its bleak and dark days contrast with the times of love, fun and sharing that reflect summer moods where everything is rosy in the fine summer sun.

Of the other two seasons in our lives, winter to spring helps us move from the difficult times to the sight of some small shoots budding, giving us hope in the future. Autumn to winter sees the opposite happening as the colours fade and the plants go into self-preservation mode. We can often find within ourselves that this is a time of feeling down or depressed. We sink deep within ourselves for self-preservation, shutting ourselves away as we are unwilling to face the days.

Life, like the countryside and our own gardens, has its ups and downs, but in all things, how we react to the changes in our lives determines whether we bloom or fade.

Gardens can be beautiful or barren. They can offer great joy and wonder, or they can bring heartache, toil and sweat. But what we experience depends on how we are in ourselves, or how we can be, in good or bad times.

Our mindset determines how we would react to circumstances. Unlike nature, which follows a pattern of spring, summer, autumn or winter, our emotions can swing in any direction or along any path as we travel through life. The thoughts of the optimist or the pessimist come to mind. Are we the type of person who sees the cup as half empty or half full? We can be positive, cheerfully looking for that brighter and better future, or we can be the doom and gloom merchant always seeing the approaching winter dullness. It all has to do with our own personal outlook on life and the choices we make. Our attitude to life and its problems are challenges for all. Some have easier lives, we agree, but it is our outlook on life and how we adapt to the changes which determine how we shape our garden of life.

I know many will look at the aspects of illness, depression and also the time and place where they were born as key factors in how life unfolds. I agree that these can make life difficult at times. However, as a person who suffers from depression and has had a few medical conditions and life circumstances that have been difficult to handle on occasions, I recognise that it is still our own decision on how we should view our situations throughout our lives. Do we blame others, blame the circumstances or do we look at life and decide to live as best we can, not letting the circumstances lead us to making the wrong choices? It is our choice which type of life to live.

Sometimes like gardening, it can be hard, toiling amid pain and sweat; but if we want to reap the benefits, we must look forward to what the future may bring. But if we are not willing to do our bit, we are then swamped among the thorns and weeds, brambles (not to mention nettles) which like a garden can choke the life out of its own being.

However, sometimes we come across a person who gives the appearance of beauty and radiance, when in fact they are anything but. Or, they live in absolute chaos all around, but they are calm and beautiful in their nature. No, life isn't easy, but in the end, it is all about how we choose to live our lives and the personal decisions we make.

The attitude and choices I speak of are clear and plain to see in the two different stories included here: the two gardens, the Garden of Eden and the Garden of Gethsemane. They outline the different types of responses we offer in our lives.

First, we have Adam (and Eve). Adam had everything. He wanted for nothing. God provided everything for him. Life was pleasant, lovely and true. All Adam had to do was to trust and believe in God for everything. The only thing God had told him not to do was to eat from the tree of knowledge. Here we see God has given Adam a choice in life. He could trust in God completely and stay away from the tree of knowledge, or he could ignore the instruction. It was his own free will. In all truth it was Eve who made the choice to eat from the tree; the choice was given to Adam, and he could have refused the offer to taste the fruit from his wife, but he chose to eat, defying God and therefore making his choice to follow his own path rather than trusting in God. God had told him he could eat of any other tree, but not the tree of knowledge. Unfortunately, like many people today, people are not content with what they have. They always want what they can never have, afford or need. Just the fact that it is out of bounds makes it desirable. Because of this, Adam and the whole human race live a life of struggle for survival with the aspect of pending death despite their hard efforts.

Second, we see Jesus. Jesus lived a life, like Adam, and he had the same choices. Jesus had every opportunity to make his own choices, every opportunity to seek to save his own life and do his own thing. However, in Gethsemane he took the road God had given him. Unlike Adam, who had been given a life of plenty and ease, Jesus was given the choice of suffering, pain even to death on the cross. At any one time Jesus could have chosen to walk away; but unlike Adam, who also had the choice to turn down the offer given by Eve, Jesus sought not to follow his will, but the will of the Father who sent him. God wanted Adam to follow his easier way, but his human weakness made him falter and then he had to face the consequences.

Jesus, on the other hand, when faced with the easier option of walking away, chose the way of God and because of this was eventually rewarded for his effort and obedience. The first Adam failed and brought mankind into disrepute with God whereas the second Adam (Jesus) repaired the error and accepted the hard road in order to pay the penalty of disobedience and allow man a way back to find God. Adam's decision was easier to make, but he made the wrong one. For Jesus, the choice was difficult as he had to select the hard way, but in the end, he chose the right path.

We all walk the walk of faith, whether we want to or not. It is called free will and we all can choose which garden we would like to live in. We have free will to walk in the world as we want, always looking out for number one (self – ego), or to seek to know the creator God and his wisdom in our lives. Some may question, is it God's way or not? But in truth this is about self – ego as we seek to blame God for everything that goes wrong in our lives. Ego, sin, whatever you want to call it, is all about self and selfish ambition. We always think that we know best and therefore walk in our own way as we will not allow others to tell us what to do. In fact, it is often the case, I have heard people say, that it was all God's fault. God should have never told Adam he had a choice. However, the flaw in that is that, otherwise, he (man) would never have free choice to follow God. We would only have been programmed to do as we were told. True love does not work that way. If we really love someone, we have to allow them to make their own choices in life, no matter how difficult it would be. The same is true in response. We often have to make difficult choices in life to show how we love someone, even at the cost to ourselves; an example would be laying down one's life for another. In Gethsemane Jesus not only laid down his own life to fulfil the will of the Father, but he gave his life as a ransom for mankind.

The best advice we can give about life's ups and downs is our analogy of the garden and a seed. A seed cannot grow unless it dies (dries out) and then it is planted in the ground. Eventually it grows and flourishes.

We are a seed planted or placed here to flourish and grow. However, if we keep ourselves and our own ambition in life for self – ego, we end up finding that our lives become empty and full of weeds. Everything and everybody seem to be getting in the way of what we think we should be. We see everyone as wrong and not part of what we want. It seems then our garden is full of weeds and thorns as the ego hides the beauty from us.

However, if we plant our seed in the master's garden, God's garden (even though it may be beside the weeds and the thorns), he will help us to grow and flourish. Our lives will truly blossom with love, care and compassion for all. Yes, weeds and thorns may try to choke us, but if we remain faithful to the Lord, we will flourish and bloom, even in the worst of times.

How do I know this?

We only have to look at the evidence. Adam (the first Adam) went along with Eve and not God. He did it his own way, and did not trust fully in God. He thought his way would be easier and more productive, having all knowledge. However, the knowledge was not just knowledge of good and loving, but also knowledge of sin and evil. This brought a darker side of nature he had never experienced before and now found himself separated from God. Adam took the aspect of his own life away from God and placed it into his own hands, and then he had to face the consequences of his actions. Separation, the struggle of life and survival became his way of life.

The second Adam (Jesus) remained faithful to the Father, no matter what the consequences. Jesus faced this decision with a clear mind and a definite aim of living his life for God rather than self (ego). Yes, he knew the evil of the world would lead to his crucifixion, a very painful death; but he knew, like the first Adam, God is the giver of life, not just physical but also eternal. The road for Jesus was never easy. It was an uphill struggle all the way, but he remained faithful as he knew it was the only real choice for self; and all mankind. He suffered, but in the end, he fully trusted in God and now reigns on high today because of his love for the Father.

Whether it is Eden or Gethsemane, we all have a garden of choice in our lives. We all have choices to make. Sometimes the garden will be delightful and peaceful, filled with love and free from cares, but often it can be hard and painful, full of sadness and disillusion. But it is how we react to life and its challenges and how and what we choose to do. Choices are never easy; they are not meant to be. Sometimes the choices may be painless and easy, but often they are hard and difficult. We have to make the right choice, not just the easiest.

You can turn the garden of peace into the garden of sorrows and separation (Eden) or the garden of peace into triumph (Gethsemane). It is all about making your own choice in life.

In the end, it is your choice to make. It is your garden of choice.

I know what garden I choose, no matter how hard it is. I choose the garden my saviour calls me to.

“Guide me O thou Great Jehovah, pilgrim through this barren land.”

I hope you make the right choice too, and that your garden of choice will be one of true love, peace, and compassion, blooming with life for all to see.

Also by this author

The Snookered Thief.

Living a Blessed Life (Non-Fiction).

The Encounter at the Viaduct and other stories.

Finding Kevin.

The Other side to No Man's Land and other stories.

In No Particular Order (Non-Fiction).

Jesus Mission, Our Commission (Non Fiction).

Why!*? (Non-Fiction).

You can contact the Author by:

Email: hiandrewmillar@hotmail.com

Facebook.

(Facebook messenger).

Printed in Poland
by Amazon Fulfillment
Poland Sp. z o.o., Wrocław

55890851R00087